ISBN- 9798843402907

copyright number: 284749339

# CONTENTS

# MR ANDERSON

**Blurb:**

*It is scandalous. It is forbidden. And yet it feels so right!*

When Willow Langly is forced to return to university after a tragic incident, the school assigns her a tutor to get her back on track. This tutor, *Mr. Anderson,* is everything Willow tries so desperately to avoid: dangerous, unpredictable and completely irresistible.

Despite the risks, Willow finds herself head over heels for the gorgeous man with the mysterious past, and very quickly learns that nothing is as it seems. As she battles her intense attraction for her tutor and the chaotic life events unravelling around her, she is forced to solve the one question she cannot answer no matter how hard she tries: who really is Mr. Anderson?

# CONTENT WARNING

Hello, Reader.

Thank you for picking up my book. Before we get started, I'd like to offer you a word of warning for what to expect in this book.

The main character of this book has a history of anxiety and depression. She suffers with severe delusions and psychosis too. Substance abuse is also mentioned. There are mental health triggers throughout, so if things like this trigger you, please proceed with caution.

Enjoy the read.

# CHAPTER ONE

## Willow's Pov:

Outside the cracked window, the squirrels scurry up a decaying tree, leaping from one crooked branch to another. Their molten gold fur shimmers under the glare of the autumn sun, a dramatic contrast to the rotting leaves beneath their tiny feet. Even from inside, I can hear them chattering to each other, noses twitching in the air every time the breeze changes directions. I imagine it's a family: mummy and daddy squirrel, closely followed by their tiny offspring. Their squeaks seem to get louder and louder, and my curiosity is piqued. What are they saying to one another? Will they share their secrets? Could they let an outcast like me join their family?

Finally, the stinging sensation in my eyes gets too much and I squeeze my eyes shut to offer some relief. The pain eases slightly, but when I reopen them, the hallucinations ramp up.

Suddenly, before my eyes, the hauntingly beautiful tree is transforming. Branches twist and turn, like hands trying to claw their way free from their bark prison; the leaves, which were once so beautifully diverse in colour, are staining a dark red that makes bile form at the back of my throat. Above, the storm rumbles ahead, blocking out the sun's gentle rays, casting threatening shadows across the meadow floor.

Mortified, I watch on as the tree starts to sing. It's an agonisingly slow tune, with a voice so haunting it leaves burn marks on my brain. A chorus of mournful sobs seeps out of it. A haunted song, for a haunted soul. It shrieks out at me, begging for me to help. *To smash the glass and free it.* If I throw my fist through this window, I could reach some of the leaves? I can save some of the tree! A bitter metallic taste burns on my tongue. The tree forces me to taste it's sorrow. I don't realise I've balled my hands into fists until I start to feel the hot familiar feel of blood trickling out under my fingernails and the dull ache in my knuckles.

*Deep breaths. It's not real. It's not plausible. Trees don't bleed or cry.* I try to repeat the calming instruction my therapist forces upon me in situations like these, but it doesn't help.

But they do. They fucking do. It's happening right now, only twenty meters away.

With a strangled sob, I squeeze my eyes tightly together, feeling every cell in my body vibrating in terror. There's a metallic taste flooding my mouth, as if the tree is forcing me to taste its sorrow again. There's a painful thumping in my head as if the squirrels are scratching their way through my skull. Their tiny, violent claws don't relent.

With a gasp, my eyes fly open. They dart to the dark tree before me, and the breath catches in my throat. My palms are clammy as I wipe them down on my trouser leg.

The tree no longer bleeds. It no longer cries. It no longer talks to me. Normality returns. Well, as much as fucking normal can get for someone with my condition.

*It is just raining,* Willow, I tell myself, but my heart doesn't stop pounding in my chest. Anxiously, I squint at the thick rain drops trickling down the tree trunk. *Yes, definitely rain.* Wide eyed, I wait for the tree to start acting up again. The relief that floods me is heavy and overwhelming. I almost forget about the other lady in the room, until her piercing voice startles me in my seat.

"Willow?" A female voice pulls me from my thoughts, "Did you hear what I just said?"

The grey-haired lady in front of me smiles sadly, her thin, red lips curving upwards, creating a ripple of lines in her tanned skin. On the lady's name tag, which is pinned to her usual white fluttery blouse, is the name *Dr Jane Dowding*.

"What tree is that?" I hear my voice ask. It doesn't sound familiar. The noise is desperate, mournful. The lady in front of me casts her gaze in the direction that I point. Her lips pull into a straight line.

"That is a Willow tree." She says after a beat. With a gulp, I nod, trying to subtly rub my sweaty palms on my trousers. My gaze catches the thin trail of blood there instead, and the lump in my throat is suffocatingly big.

As if sensing my discomfort, Dr Dowding folds one long leg over the other, and leans closer.

"How does that make you feel?" She asks quizzically. "That it has the same name as you, that is…?"

I look at her blankly. This is the kind of question you'd ask a traumatised child, not a twenty-two-year-old. My jaw clenches as I avoid eye contact.

When the silence stretches into two full minutes, she finally gives up, and slumps back in her seat.

"We should talk about the day of the fire." She tells me. Her lips twitch upwards into a friendly smile. I don't return it. The lump in my throat worsens. Looking for a distraction, I peer back out of the window. The furry little animals have disappeared, and the tree is being battered side to side in the gale. A chill rocks through my body as if I am one with the tree. Both of us are trying to withhold the assault of the howling wind.

"I'm not ready yet." I whisper. Finally, I tear my gaze away from the tree. My vision blurs as the tears threaten to spill down my face again.

"It's been six months, Willow." She pushes gently, "And whilst I'm happy to go as slowly as you'd like in these sessions, I'm nervous that we haven't made any real progress. Especially with the new academic year starting in a couple of days."

I catch a sob in my mouth as I pull my legs to my chest, hugging them protectively. I dropped out of University last term due to my depression swallowing me up. All I could do was cry and hug my pillow. And it's all I still can do. And now I must return to the gawping eyes and bitter rumours.

"*Look!*" They will say, "*That's the orphan! That's the girl who jumped out of a burning building and left her parents behind.*"

"*Did you hear she started the fire?*" They will add, "*Oh, yes. She's crazy that one! She's been insane since primary school, but now she's a murderer! She should be locked away!*"

I choke on the thoughts, convinced my own body is trying to shut itself down.

"Willow?" The doctor raises a concerned eyebrow. I lean forward in my seat, and it feels as if time has sped up. It has a funny way of doing this. Sometimes it slows down, other times it's as if I can feel the seconds pouring through my fingers. No matter how frantically I grasp, and I grasp, I am helpless. It feels like only a couple of days ago the tragedy struck this small town. And yet here I am, half a year later, being forced back into education. Where time won't fucking stay still.

"I promise I'll open up next session." I tell her uncertainly.

*Lie.* My fingers itch for a cigarette; my chapped lips automatically pinch, as if I'm inhaling one now. I try to flex my aching hands, but the desire doesn't go away.

I *need* the distraction. Doctor Jane doesn't let me smoke in here anymore. *It's a bad habit,* she says, *a destructive habit.* And yet she will help herself to one at least once a session.

With a sharp inhale of breath, I force my eyes to meet the doctors.

"You say that every week." My doctor scowls at me. She peers down at the session report in her lap and flicks through my folder. Her mouth tightens into a miserable, straight line as I resist the urge to get up and flee. She's right. I say this every week. I just wished she got the message. Not every trauma needs to be spoken about. Not every trauma needs to be relived.

I remain quiet, silently challenging her. She knows that if she pushes too much I will just shut down. And I am on the verge of having a silent spell for a couple days. My words are like mud between my lips. It's too horrible to spit them out because the grit and dirt will get caught in your teeth, but even worse to keep it in. I just want it all to stop. The therapy. The pressure. *My life.*

"Let us talk about your academia." She changes the subject, pulling out a document from the bundle of papers.

"Unfortunately, you missed four months off school, and this caused a huge drop in your grades. We've already spoken in the past about the importance of you attending your lessons this year and doing well, otherwise the university will de-fund your scholarship." She explains, waving her hands around. I slump back further in the chair.

"The university doesn't want to make you re-sit the year. It will be too stressful for you, and you've almost finished your degree now. So, as we've discussed in the past, you will be learning last year's materials alongside this years. Your examination will be at Christmas to see whether you've passed." The therapist continues, "To help you, the university has kindly given you a tutor. He will be the person you report to and have extra sessions with. How does this sound?"

As I choke on a sob, I shake my head. The mass of information is too much, even if she has been repeating this same nonsense for the last two months straight. I can't avoid university. It is my way out of this small town. But there is no way in Hell I will face those spiteful rumours. People can be such assholes surrounding trauma. It's as if it is worse for them rather than the actual victim.

"Willow, come on, you have to try." My doctor scolds, the smile on her face faltering. I clear my throat and readjust my position in the large chair. Silently, I pray for it to swallow me up.

"Sorry, yes, that sounds good." I stutter, trying to sound grateful. Again, I don't recognise my own voice. I have never sounded this miserable. This helpless. My doctor offers me a tight smile.

"Okay." She says unconvinced, "Oh, and your tutor is called Professor Anderson."

A long pause drifts between us. I finally break the silence.

"Is he new?"

"Yes. Good catch." She beams.

"This is a new start for you Willow. A new year, a new professor, perhaps new friends? It's time for you to fight your depression and have the happy life your parents would have wanted." She explains, waving her glasses around.

The air in my mouth goes stale and I spit it out.

*There...* She said it. *'The happy life your parents would have wanted'* those famous fucking words. Why does every Therapist and nosy neighbour think that these words will fix the black hole within my heart? It's not that fucking simple! Nobody understands what it is like to have this type of shadow attached to your back. It's not something you can just shake off. It's not something you can just avoid. No, it's here forever. No matter what Doctor Jane or anyone else thinks.

Trying to distract myself, I glance towards the clock on the wall. I'm surprised to see it's a different one to usual, it's red and the design makes it look like it's melting off the wall.

For a moment, my whole body goes still.

Wait a moment... *is it the design or is it actually melting off the wall?*

Subconsciously, my fingers grip onto the armchair to steady my trembling body. My heart skips a beat as I blink once. Twice. However, the fucking clock doesn't change.

*What is happening? Is it the design? Is it going to fall off the wall? Melting? The design? Is it melting? The des-*

Shakily, I try my breathing exercises, but the fucking clock doesn't change. *What is happening? Is it the design? Is it going to fall off the wall? Is it the design? Melting? The design? Is it melting? The des-*

"Oh, Willow!" My doctor gasps as she flies to her feet. Panicked, she rushes over and pulls the clock down off the wall, tucking it hastily behind her back.

"Sorry, I completely forgot I had this here. I had a child in before you which explains the colours around the room. They liked this clock and the design..." She apologises. A breath sneaks into my lungs. I have my answer. For once, it wasn't my psychosis. I give the room a half look before averting my gaze towards the navy, carpeted floor. The simple design is easier to comprehend.

"Well, you know, you weren't supposed to be here today and... Well, it doesn't matter now, does it?" She offers me a half smile. I resist the urge to roll my eyes. She is right- my brother booked me an emergency appointment an hour ago. Apparently twice a week isn't good enough. I had to see her this morning too.

"Speaking of that, how *is* your psychosis?" She sinks back into her chair, still clutching the clock. I feel like if I tried hard enough I could look *through* here and see the fucking thing.

"Good." I lie.

"Willow." She sighs, "You can tell me the truth. I am here to help you, not to harm you. If you open up about these things, we can work on it together. Only then can we create coping mechanisms to..."

"The session is over." I bark, cutting her off. My voice is harsher than I mean it to be, but I don't care. I cannot stand another second in this fucking room. I feel the temper rising in my chest. Again, my emotions get the better of me. They come and go so quickly I can't catch them. Just like time, they are slippery motherfuckers.

"Yes." My doctor says quietly, "Yes, it is. Okay well you have a great first day at University on Monday. I will see you within the week to catch up."

I can't answer her. It feels as though I've lost my voice.

"Oh, and Willow?" She adds, "Make sure you go and introduce yourself to Mr Anderson, he will be expecting you!"

Despair fills me.

Slowly, I nod my head but in the back of my mind, I know that I will not be showing up to the scheduled tuition sessions. I do not need any more help. If I am going to be forced to attend university again, I can do it alone, like I do with every other thing in my life.

# CHAPTER TWO

## Willow's Pov:

*She's here.*

She is standing there. In the corner of my room, my mother's tarred body leans against the door. One leg is propped up against the wall and her arms are crossed over her chest menacingly. I feel the smoke around her seep into my lungs, like snakes crawling up my nose, tumbling down into my chest and then dying there. Her head cocks to the side as she watches me. Then, she moves.

"No, mum!" I cry out as she takes a step closer. She has no hair on her head, it has all been burnt off from the fire. Her skin peels back, revealing bone and fleshy tissues. She used to be so beautiful, and now, she looks like a demon from Hell. My stomach lurches as her hands reach out towards me.

"Mum please!" I beg her, "Stop! Just stop it!"

I can't stand it! She visits me every night, haunts my nightmares. The fear grips my body and I tremble. Suddenly, my father joins her side. His eyes are sunken and face half melted off. My mother definitely had been burnt worse, but he is just as hideous.

"You left us!" My mother's chipped voice echoes around the room, "You left us to die in the fire!"

"It is all your fault!" My father's booming voice overpowers her. I lunge forwards. The smoke is cramming into my lungs, suffocating me. Hot flames scorch my skin as sweat starts to pool at the back of my collar. Suddenly the room is alight with flames. My lungs scream in agony as does my peeling flesh.

"No, please! Stop it! Stop it!" I shriek but it doesn't work. If anything, my mother makes the fire worse. It licks at my skin and turns my bones charcoal.

My father explodes with anger, "You caused the fire! And then left! Fucking left! Left us!"

He charges towards me and grabs me by my throat. I scratch at his face, but he can't feel it. All his nerves have been burnt off. He usually reminds me of this gruesome fact halfway through the struggle. His grip tightens and tightens until I feel my head on the edge of exploding. It's an agony like never before. Except, it happens every night.

"Willow?" A voice calls out to me. I can't make out the other person in the flames.

"Willow, you have to wake up!" My brother's panicked voice rings through the room. He races through the flames and suddenly everything disappears.

No more flames. No more parents. No more suffocating.

Startled, I shoot upwards in bed and throw myself against the headboard. The sweat clings to my body and exhaustion seeps into my bones. I feel even worse than when I got into bed. Jake's eyes soften when he notices my distress.

"Another bad dream?" He grimaces, placing the back of his hand to my forehead. At the heat, he swears softly under his breath and yanks it free. However, I don't have the energy to answer him. With a small unsteady breath, I sink back into my bed, yanking the covers up to my chin. My body begs me to cry, but I can't. I have no more tears left. I just need five minutes of actual sleep.

My brother doesn't give me the luxury.

"You slept through the alarm." His pity vanishes when I give him the cold shoulder. Instead, he strides across the room, strategically dodging the piles of worn clothes and sealed carboard boxes which I haven't had the energy to open since we moved. Then, he thrusts the curtains open and an onslaught of light fills the room around me. Miserably, I groan and pull the pillow over my head, but he quickly removes it.

"Get up, now!" He barks at me.

"No!"

His patience thins, "Willow, get up!"

I risk a peek at his expression to see whether I could worm my way out of this, but his face is flushed and tense. Dark rings hang under his own eyes and a light shadow of stubble stains his face. I want to resist and slip back into a deep sleep, but the wild look in his eyes removes any idea of resistance. With a look of disgust, he casts his gaze around the room.

"And pick up all this shit. How can you live like this?"

I don't follow his gaze, knowing exactly what hell-hole I'd find. Despite using all our inheritance to buy this two-bedroom apartment, it's tiny, and there is barely any space to put things away. Hence, the floordrobe was born.

"I will clean it up tonight." I promise him but its half-hearted. If I had it my way, there wouldn't be an inch of floor to be seen. Who has the energy to tidy up when you can't even convince yourself to eat or shower?

Jake frowns at me for a long moment, but then relents, "Fine. But I will hold you to that promise. Now, get up. Your first lesson starts soon."

I hesitate, and this sends him over the edge.

"Please, Willow." He begs me, voice strained and tense, "I know you didn't sleep well, and I'm sorry that you're still suffering with these dreams but…"

"But what?" I hiss angrily, "But I should open up at therapy? That I should attend University with all the pitiful stares? That I should *try*? Is that what you're going to say, Jake? I know! I fucking know what I have to do! I just *can't*!"

As soon as the words leave my lips, I regret them. The sad look in his eyes causes the pain in my chest to start; I swallow back all the bite and adrenaline coursing through my veins, fixing him with an apologetic look instead.

My emotions are everywhere. *Uncontrollable.* The helplessness claws at my heart. Although the thought of attending University is bad, making my brother upset is much worse. He is the only thing I have left, and I cannot ruin it. Between working day and night, he has been working hard to keep us afloat and eating. The plan was always for him to keep us alive *now*, and then when I finish University, I will secure us a higher paying job and help out as well. However, as my body slumps further into the mattress we had found near the dumpsters, I want to protest and refuse to do my part of the plan. But I won't. I have to do this for him. For us.

"I'm sorry." I whisper, pushing myself into a sitting position. Jake shakes it off. He rarely acknowledges my outbursts anymore. Instead, he heads towards the pile of clothes in a carboard box. A simple look. We couldn't afford much when we had to buy a whole new wardrobe. He places it on the bed next to me.

"Wear this. Your bag is already packed downstairs. We leave in five minutes." He says sternly before exiting the room. Not wanting to piss him off any further, I race to put the clothes on. I quickly brush my teeth and try to brush my hair with my fingers. The dark knotty tendrils resist against my touch. A miserable, pale looking woman stares back at me in the cracked, bathroom mirror. Her lips are dark, but the rest of her skin resembles chalk. Long black eyelashes dancing around those haunted eyes; the eyes which lost a couple shades of colour as she jumped from a burning building. Black eyes for a black soul.

And then they change. The dark eyes now seem to swirl and burst into flames. My face feels scorched by the fire. A thin layer of sweat licks at the back of my neck. Again, mournful cries echo around me. I throw my hands to my ears and try to force the images out of my mind. It doesn't help.

*Deep breaths. Deep breaths. Deep breaths.*

Horrified, I watch as my hair falls off my head, scorched from the fire. A black tar coats my skin now and I can see the smoke. The roars of flames join the onslaught, closely followed by a dark smoke fogging up the bathroom. It stinks of burning flesh.

"No." I hear myself whimper. The sound is quiet. *Desperate.* I drop to my knees and choke on the smoke around me. My lungs constrict in agony as I gasp for oxygen. There isn't any. The smoke fills my lungs.

"Willow!" My brother hollers from downstairs.

Suddenly, everything stops. No more smoke, no more choking, no more fire. Before the room can change again, I snap into action and charge down the stairs and out the door. I have no time to pity myself. I have no right to either. Because of my actions, my parents are dead. The delusions and nightmares are simply karma. I deserve these, and more.

"Yes, Yes. I'm here." I pant, throwing myself into the rusty, scarlet car. A neighbour had offered it to us after the incident. Their son had passed his driving test and moved on to get a frighteningly expensive new car. We happily accepted this run-around vehicle which would probably concave if we got into a crash.

My brother's lips pull into a grim line as he throws the car into gear. I shiver and try to catch my breath.

"I will not be doing this every morning, Willow!" Jake hisses as we hit a sharp corner. The tyres of the car shriek against the tarmac. I clutch onto the handle and desperately try to stay upright.

"I'll be on time tomorrow, I promise." I lie. Deep down, we both know I will pull the same trick every morning. I am not going to attend University easily.

"Now, I'm going to be late to work too." He grumbles. The sound of indicators echoes around the car as Jake signals into the University car park. We are only a couple of minutes' drive away from the university, so it isn't a particularly long journey. Yet the guilt pulls at me. I am making my brother's life much harder just by being resistant.

"I'm sorry, Jake." I whisper. Almost instantly, his face softens.

"It's okay, just please, let's not make a thing out of this. I can't be late every morning. They are already looking at firing a couple people to keep costs low. And as I'm fairly new there and inexperienced, I fear it might be me." His jaw hardens as he spins the car into a parking space. I lurch to the side and quickly readily myself. I nod my head understandingly.

"Yes, I promise. No more problems." I tell him with certainty. Jake looks in the back seat and then at me.

"Did you grab your bag from the kitchen counter?" He frowns. I stiffen in my seat. Anxiousness fills me as I bite my lower lip.

"No." I confess. My brother's grip on the steering wheel tightens and I watch as he slowly loses his cool.

"I'm sorry, Jake! I'm working on it, okay? I'm sorry that I am late. I'm sorry that I forgot! It's been a while, okay?" I rant angrily. He doesn't answer me. My heart races one hundred miles an hour.

"Thank you for the lift." I tell him before jumping out of the car to avoid his rage.

"Have a good day, Willow." He calls after me. Relief fills me. He's not picking a fight because he understands. *I think.* That or he doesn't have the energy to fight.

I check my watch as I start racing towards the large, Victorian building. The second bell goes, confirming my suspicions that

I'm late. I march up the corridor and round to the left, searching for the building I studied in last year. I skid to a halt outside a blue-looking door. Peering in through the small glass frame, my heart flutters in my chest. The lecture hall is empty.

*Wrong classroom.*

Another wave of helplessness fills me. I pull out my phone and desperately search down my emails, searching for the welcome email to locate the room. I can't find it. I stumble down the hallway and glance into each room. This is the English block, so it has to be around here somewhere.

After what feels like an eternity, I arrive outside a dark door. Quickly, I slip inside and stare up at the dozens of blank faces staring toward the front of the classroom. It is almost deadly silent as I scurry up the lecture hall stairs towards a free seat at the back.

"Wait!" A booming voice stops me dead in my tracks. I take a couple deep breaths before turning around. I desperately try to decipher whether it is a hallucination or real. I can't be making a fool of myself on my first day. And reality feels quite hazy this week. My therapist told me when I am unsure, I can check other people's reactions. If they all react, then I'm most likely interacting with something real.

Nervously, I peer around. Every face in the lecture hall turns to face me. I feel myself turn a couple shades darker. *Fuck, it's real.* Something inside of me wishes it was just an illusion.

"Yes?" I squeak. My world feels fuzzy and it's almost as if I can hear every single conversation within the lecture hall. The poorly whispered rumours being passed between each person.

At the front of the hall, a man in his late thirty's stares back at me. He is stunning with raven-coloured, slicked back hair and sharp features. Dark eyes watch me, and his plump lips pull into a grim line. A groomed beard also clings to his beautiful face. My fingers itch to touch it for some strange reason.

"Who do we have here?" He asks smugly, walking towards my side of the room. I tremble as a chorus of snickers echo around.

"Willow Langly, Sir." I answer. He cocks his head to the side. Those piercing eyes never leave me.

"Care to explain why you are fifteen minutes late to my lecture?" He demands. As he folds his arms across his chest, his large muscles threaten to jump out of his tight black shirt. I avert my eyes to the floor.

"I overslept." I say lamely.

"You overslept?" He scoffs, rolling his eyes. My cheeks flush a darker shade of red.

"And where is your laptop to take notes?" He scowls. I bite my lower lip nervously. *Burnt in a house fire,* I want to say. Instead, I shake my head,

"I don't have a laptop."

His eyebrows burrow together on his forehead as he frowns harder. A long, awkward silence drifts between us. I feel my entire body tremble in humiliation. His inscrutable look turns to smugness, as if he enjoys my anxiety.

Another wave of laughter echoes in the audience. His face hardens and he glares in the direction of the sound. Then, he suddenly spins on his heel and marches toward his desk.

He rips at his notepad, tearing off a couple pages of paper before taking the pen from his desk and turning towards me. The sound of the tearing echoes around the room, and I gulp, silently praying the floor will swallow me whole. Shakily, I meet him halfway on the stairs.

"Here you go, Miss Langly." He says quieter this time so that only I can hear him. My name on his lips stirs something in my chest, but I push the feeling away quickly. He hands me the pen and paper.

"Thank you." I whisper. I keep my gaze locked firmly on the

ground, afraid that if I make eye contact, I will pass out from humiliation. Nonetheless, I can feel his gaze firmly locked on me. I am the sheep, and he is the wolf. We both know how this story will end.

"Please take a seat. I'm afraid you've missed the introductions but I'm sure you'll catch up." He instructs me more calmly this time. Then, he turns to continue with his lecture. As soon as he finishes his sentence, I scurry up the stairs and hide towards the back of the lecture hall.

I choose a seat away from the other students and force myself to take normal breaths. The adrenaline pumps through me and I feel sick. My humiliation turns to anger. *How dare he try and humiliate me like that in front of everybody? Does he get an enjoyment from embarrassing people on their first day of class? Who does he think he is?*

"Everyone, please turn to chapter one of your book." He booms from the front of the class. His eyes flicker over to me. And for a moment, I see another smirk pull at his lips. He knows I don't have the book. A sinking feeling stirs in my stomach. The anger switches back to humiliation.

"If you do not have the book 'One that flew over the cuckoo's nest' please come to the front. I have a couple of spare copies here." He offers, heading towards his desk and holding up the spare copies he promised. A couple students awkwardly get up and make their way toward him. Cheeks stained red, I sink further into my chair, hoping I can get away with not having a physical copy of the book today. The idea of having to go back over to him makes my palms sweaty.

As if he can read my mind, the professor turns to face me again. After a long thirty seconds, I realise he's waiting for me to approach. He silently dares me to ignore his instruction so he can further humiliate me.

My face is hot as I slowly rise from my seat and make my way back down the steps. Each step I take feels like one closer to my death. I still clutch the paper and pen, afraid that if I put them down, I might lose them and have to ask more off of the professor. When I'm finally in front of him, he thrusts the book into my hands but doesn't let go as I try to pull back.

"Perhaps you should sit at the front." He tells me with an evil flicker in his eyes, "That way you won't have to keep going up and down those stairs each time you need something from me."

A mortified squeak falls from my lips, "Yes, sir."

His nostrils flare, and those dark eyes burn onto my face. I quickly cast my eyes down to his hands on the book, silently begging him to release it. His knuckles turn white from the vice-like grip, but I'm more taken aback by how large his hands are. They are almost twice the size of mine. I gulp.

"Go." He grunts the single word before releasing the book. *Dismissing* me. My eyes prick with tears from the humiliation as I scurry to the seat at the front. Despite all my best efforts to distract myself with flicking through the book, I can feel that taunting gaze still attached to me. Licking up every emotion that floods through me. I've only known him fifteen minutes, but one thing is clear: he enjoys my discomfort. Making me feel powerless. But what he doesn't know is that I had no power to begin with. Let him torment me, perhaps its just another way the universe is punishing me.

# CHAPTER THREE

## Willow's Pov:

Counter to my prayers, the class passes slowly, the distant chatter of the classroom blurs into white noise around me as I scan through my book silently. Before the fire, I was an avid reader. My mother used to scold me for losing track of reality as I cuddled up in bed, reading through endless amounts of literature. Since her death, I found it incredibly difficult to return to reading. *Time might go by too fast. I might miss events. I might regret wasting time later on.*

The bell shrieks around the room. I jolt and grip the table violently. The loud noise frightens me, and I feel the hairs on the back of my neck stand to attention. Shakily, I try to steady my breathing. The room around me erupts into chaos as the students shoot out of their chairs and pack up their things. It makes my anxiety worse. I'm frozen in my seat, staring at the book in front of me. It snaps itself shut and loses my page. Even my only distraction flees.

"Okay, thank you, everybody. Please read up to page 54 before the next session. You may leave." The professor declares to the class. Out of the corner of my eye, I watch him, not that his eyes aren't locked on me.

He gently places his book on his desk before twisting to face the scattering students. A proud look floods through his face as he nods his head, acknowledging the 'thank you's' that some students mutter. I don't miss the way he makes his eyes twinkle, and how he curves his lips into a smile on cue. The mask is *very* convincing, but I know a mask when I see one. He seems less intense when looking at other people, and I suppose you could say quite handsome. What am I saying? He is *very* handsome in a rugged sort of way. Like he embodies the word *danger* and *safety* at once, if that is even possible. I've always had a thing for dark features. It's as if the darkness within me is attracted to theirs. And this professor seems to ooze darkness, though he hides it well.

Then, his gaze finds mine and the mask is dropped. His lips curve downward in disgust, almost as if I've reminded him of a chore. *Time to go,* the rational voice in my head squeaks. Frantically, I scramble to my feet and gather up all the loose sheets of paper with only three notes on it in total.

He senses my desperation.

"Miss Langly." He calls out my name, and it sends dread through me. I pretend not to hear him and shrug my coat on quickly before exiting the row of seats. But he moves faster than I could have anticipated.

Suddenly, he is right in front of me, glaring down at me like a scolded child. He holds his hands out, ready to physically stop me if I try to escape. It makes me stumble backward in shock. Surely, he wouldn't grab me, *right*? That would be unprofessional. Professors can't grab their students. Surely not.

"Miss Langly." He drawls and for a second, I think he is about to start tutting, "I am talking to you."

The lump in my throat starts throbbing painfully.

"Sorry, I didn't hear you." I squeak, not missing the way he arches a disapproving eyebrow at me. For a moment, his lip twitches upward into a smug grin, but he drops it quickly. He is less than two steps away from me, and I can feel his hot breath on my face when he talks.

"Sit down." He commands, not moving an inch. Instead, he

waits patiently for me to obey him. And much to my despair, my traitorous body stumbles toward the nearest seat and forces me into it. With a small smile, he blinks, releasing me from his intense stare.

"Good." He says with a nod, "Now, let me introduce myself since you rudely missed the first part of my lecture. First things first, you will address me as Mr Anderson." He says, grabbing a whiteboard pen and marching toward the large board behind him. The pen shrieks as he carves out each letter of his name before underlining it twice. His hand flexes around it, and almost swallows it whole.

"Am I understood?" He notices my silence and spins around to gauge my reaction. I have to force my lips to stay locked together or else my jaw might swing open from shock. This might be the most unprofessional professor I have ever had.

*Does he know why I am here? Does he know my backstory?* Surely, my doctor would have contacted him and informed him. And yet here he is, with zero pity. I lean back in my chair, trying to muster some confidence. He prays on weaknesses. I shouldn't give it to him so freely. Deep down, I know this is what I need. What I *want*. No tip toeing around. No small, pitiful smiles and reassuring words. I have therapy twice a week to heal. I'm here to learn. And I have no doubt that Mr Anderson will ensure it.

"Miss Langly?" He presses. I jump into action to avoid further conflict.

"Yes, sir. I, er, mean, Mr. Anderson."

His jaw tenses disapprovingly.

"I am your new tutor, much to both of our displeasure. This is going to be equally unpleasant and tedious for both of us, but it must be done so you pass your exams at Christmas. So, I'd appreciate it if you attended *on time*, and had some enthusiasm for learning."

He curls his lip in disgust, and it makes me physically pull back in shock. I itch to ask him why he is teaching me if he doesn't want to, but Mr. Anderson doesn't strike me as the type of man to reveal answers. Only ask questions. I nod my head to pretend I'm listening, not trusting my words to not make a fool of myself.

"Right," He sighs, looking at his watch and then back at me, "Let us start the first lesson then. Get it over and done with."

"Now?" I squeak in shock.

"Yes, unless you have somewhere else to be?" He frowns. Slowly, he crosses his arms over his chest and watches me with a raised eyebrow. He dares me to say *no* to him. Humiliation fills me. *Of course, I have no plans.* Well, other than going home and sleeping the day away.

"That's what I thought." He hums to himself, "We will see each other two to three times a week until your exams at Christmas." He turns to face me with a grim expression, "Which days' work best for you?"

Before I can answer, he opens his mouth to talk again.

"I think we should have our sessions straight after the timetabled lectures." He states. I nod my head slowly. His eyes home in on me for a second too long before he snatches his attention to the blank sheet of paper in front of him. He picks it up and marches towards me. I flinch. He moves too fast. He is too unpredictable. And now he is far too close.

The smell of cigarettes and oak fills my nose and a weird sensation floods through me. My head feels light, and I almost feel drunk. Unaware of the effect on me, he thrusts the paper in my face. I try to take it, but yet again, he doesn't release it. He twists his hand slightly and it makes it awkward for me to hold. But at this angle, I notice a large, jagged scar on this thumb. The skin pinches up and around his knuckle, stopping where his nail starts. It's red and looks fairly new. Noticing my gaze, he snaps it away, releasing the paper.

"Right." He clears his throat, "First task. I want to see your writing skills." He explains. His eyes don't meet mine anymore, and I watch as his Adam's apple bobs as he swallows hard, "Write me a short story about your life. It can be about anything and in any format."

I bite my lower lip nervously as I stare down at the blank piece of paper in front of me. *What would I write about? What topic is suitable for this? What could I write about without revealing too much about myself?*

"Do you have anything in mind?" He prods.

"No, professor."

He corrects me sharply, "It's Mr Anderson to you."

"No, Mr Anderson. I do not have anything in mind." I can't help the way I slur my words in frustration to his cold attitude. He cocks an eyebrow at my retort and a challenging look flickers across his face. I instantly regret my words.

"Well, think of something." He says unhelpfully, "Or else it will be ungradable and you will fail. Not a great way to start our sessions, don't you think?"

*Twat.* He knows he is winding me up. My jaw hardens and I sink my teeth into my tongue to keep my anger in check. It brims to the surface, wanting to escape, but I force my unpredictable rage down.

"It can be about anything, Willow. I don't care what. A pet, a memory, an event. Be creative."

His advice doesn't help. I nod my head, desperately trying to conjure up something creative. But my brain is blocked under his intense gaze.

"Professor." A voice from the corner of the room calls out. My head snaps up in the direction of the red-haired woman. She wears a tiny black dress with fishnet tights and long, studded boots. She has a little button nose that has been powdered with a red blush, which contrasts the thick eyeliner that shoots off of her round, blue eyes. Her eyes are fixed on Mr. Anderson.

"Olivia! Nice to see you again. How may I help?" He plasters a fake smile to his lips.

She gets straight to the point, "I need help on an assignment question. Can we have a chat outside about it?"

He frowns at her, and I find myself frowning too. What assignment? We've only just began the term, which horrid professors are already setting essays? Mr Anderson opens his mouth to protest but she quickly cuts him off

"Like, *now.*"

It snaps him into action for whatever reason, "Yes, yes, of course."

As he walks toward the door, he waves a hand dismissively at me, "I will be back in twenty minutes, Willow. Write as much as you can. Make it good."

*Twenty minutes?* I scowl. *What could they be talking about for twenty minutes?* And what could I write about for twenty minutes?

I don't miss her failed whisper as he closes the door behind him.

*"Was that your tutee?"* She asked. What is it to her? Why does she need to know that? An uneasy feeling pulls through me, but I try to shake it off. Today has been a very long and confusing day. Perhaps I misheard. Perhaps I hallucinated it.

Bored, I turn my attention back to the mocking blank piece of paper. Now that Mr Anderson's overwhelming presence is gone, I relax slightly.

I mentally flick through my childhood, deciding that this is the easiest thing to write about. Not many things jump out at me without being tarnished with guilt for my parents' deaths. But then one does.

I remember the summer holiday with my family by the beach in southern France a couple years back. It is my favourite holiday we had together. We spent every day in the water, playing on inflatable toys which were pulled by the boat we rented out. A smile tugs at my lips at the memory. I remember the countless fish and chips we had, the endless laughs and the closeness I felt towards my family. The salty air drying out our lips out and sticking in our hair. My mum bought us each a ChapStick to help with it but that caused more problems. ChapStick, alongside sun cream, had been a recipe for hair disasters when the warm breeze would throw your hair into the sticky stuff. I remember my mum pulling me and my brother close into an embrace. Her warm vanilla smell filled my nostrils. *"I love you two."* She whispered to us, *"No matter what happens between me and your father, we are family. We will always love you."*

That was five years ago. At the time, I was unaware of my parent's martial issues. Mum was so cryptic with it, and Dad was distant around her. *Guilty* around her. And yet on that holiday, it was as if we were a normal family again. I shudder.

I haven't thought about that holiday for a while now.

Only now that the air is back in my lungs, I release my pen is moving frantically. I don't think I have ever written so fast and yet so beautifully. A tear slips down my cheek. Time quickly passes by as the ink flows out of my pen. It's like a weight has been lifted off my chest as I write all my thoughts and feelings down.

"Okay, how is it going?" Mr Anderson asks as he strides back into the room. I jolt at the sudden interruption. Quickly, I wipe the tear from my face. A fake smile jumps to my lips as I push my work towards him. Wide eyed, he stares down at scribbled writing on three sides of A4. I don't even care about his reaction. All that matters is the warm feeling bubbling in my stomach. In that moment, the loving side of my mum was there with me, guiding me as I described my favourite holiday. It was a stark contrast to the usual nightmare surrounding her. *The fire. The screams. The torture.*

I tense up and protectively hug my body. An anxiousness fills me. I almost regret offering him this insight into my life. He is a stranger, a stranger who will now judge my thoughts and feelings. My fingers shoot out to grab the work, but he snatches it away with a stern look. He slowly heads toward his desk and leans against it before he scans the documents carefully.

I feel nervous as his eyebrows do all the talking. They shoot upwards, scowl downwards and become motionless. They repeat this little dance for too long. More and more nerves seep into my chest. I scold myself for not proof reading. For not checking grammatical and spelling errors. I was so lost in the story. I forgot the task. *Damn.* Nervously, I wait for the inevitable criticisms.

"Willow..." He trails off, shaking his head in disbelief, "This is amazing. The detail, the structure, the *content*..."

My mouth hangs open, but I quickly snap it shut. Instead, I fiddle with the pen in my fingers anxiously.

"It is fascinating that you chose a poem structure. It's like I'm there." He compliments again, bringing the paper away from his face to look at me, "You have talent. Now we just need you to be motivated and bring you up to speed with the course material. I have no doubt that you will excel."

"Thank you." I squeak.

Our eyes meet and it's as if a spell has been cast. I feel as though I'm falling into those dark irises, and I'm not even mad about it. The darkness comforts me, excites me. My tongue darts out and I subconsciously dampen my lips. His low eyes catch the movement, and something flickers across his face. Hunger? Surely not. No, I must be seeing things.

"Let's turn to last year's material." He clears his throat, letting the pieces of paper fall to the desk. I don't answer him, afraid that if I use my voice, it will sound weak. Desperate. *Crazy.*

He doesn't look at me as he opens the textbook and begins writing things on the board. A nagging feeling pulls at the bottom of my chest. And yet I can't put my finger on what it's saying. And it's not like I can ask him whether that look was real or just a figment of my imagination. My crazy fucking imagination.

# CHAPTER FOUR

## Willow's Pov:

Numbness fills me as I stare at the blinds on the window. Today, I am not allowed to look at the squirrels. Today, I am not allowed to have the luxury of such distractions.

"How has your week been?" Doctor Jane asks me. My head feels heavy as I turn to look at her.

"I don't like my tutor." I confess, "I want another one."

Doctor Jane's eyebrows pull together in shock. She brings the clipboard to her chest as she scoots closer to me.

"What? Why? Mr Anderson is a lovely man." She protests. I look at her blankly. It doesn't matter what I say, he is sane, and I am diagnosed as crazy. He will win this argument.

"It's only been a week, Willow. You need to give him more time than that." She frowns at me, "What makes you dislike him?"

My mouth parts slowly. Could I tell her that I think my professor is hot and that it makes me nervous? That he is an arrogant asshole who gets off on making me blush? How I've only had one session with him, but this is one too many. He insults me, humiliates me, and then every now and then I find myself looking at his lips, wondering what they taste like?

 Shaking my head, I turn my attention back to the blinds.

"Can we open them?" I ask. Doctor Jane doesn't answer me, so I begin to climb out of my chair.

"Willow." She snaps, "Sit down. You're avoiding the question."

"I just want to see the squirrels." I tell her defensively. But I do as she says and remain in my seat. Then, I pull my legs to my chest protectively and let my chin rest on my knees. I take a couple deep breaths to steady my anxiety. My therapist watches me curiously.

"You seem more in touch with reality." She says as if it's a good thing. I blink away the burning tears. *It is true.* I slept surprisingly well this week. I had one night of uninterrupted sleep! Jake told me it's because I've been exhausted with the week of University. I think it's because mum helped me through that writing task. It was a step closer to healing. A step I took *without* the help of anyone else. Just another reason why therapy and tuition are a waste of money, time and effort.

The thought of my mother brings her to life. Suddenly, she is standing behind Doctor Jane. With melting eyes, she watches me. Though I cannot see her iris', I feel that scrutinising gaze. She doesn't say anything, but her crossed arms and rigid stance says enough. I gulp as I look at her. Today, her dark hair tumbles down her back. Each tendril floats around her face as if she is submerged under water. She wears a long, tarred nightdress. It falls to the floor and covers her feet. Thank goodness. Usually, her toes are burnt off- it's terrifying.

"Reality scares me." I confess quietly before I can stop myself. My mother cocks her head to the side, and I feel her gaze grow more intense.

My therapist gawps at me.

"Go on. What are you scared about?" She presses gently. I can see the excitement bubbling inside of her. She thinks that this is a breakthrough. My eyes remain fixed on my mother. I wait for her to attack. She never usually waits this long before hurting me. Before seeking revenge.

"The more I engage with reality, the harder it is to decipher the difference between fantasy. Doctor, I am struggling to know what is real and what is not. *Again*." I spit out. Something in my finger burns me. My attention snaps to the lit cigarette in my fingers. *When did I light that? When did the doctor allow me to smoke again?* Slowly, I lean forward and put it out in the cigarette pot.

My head snaps up, but my mother is gone. Frightened, I toss my gaze left and right, knowing she usually disappears before attacking.

*Where is that slippery bitch? How will she hurt me today?*

"Have you got any examples?" Doctor Jane regains my attention. I can tell she is resisting the urge to scribble all these notes down. The last time I began to open up, and she wrote it down, I grew quiet again.

I look at the cigarette burning away in the box and then I think back to the bleeding tree. The smoke in the bathroom. My mother appearing during the day. The hungry look in my professor's eyes. A nervousness fills my body with that last one. I peer up at my doctor helplessly and shake my head.

"No." I whisper.

"Willow." She purses her lips together, "You know I can't help you unless you open up."

I challenge her with a long silence. Eventually, she sighs and rocks back in her seat.

*The breakthrough is over.*

"Okay, so you're experiencing severe psychosis and delusions again. And are you taking your medication properly?" She raises an eyebrow up at me. My face contorts as I think about the little red pills which are hard to swallow. They get stuck in your throat and leave you with a painful lump for the rest of the day. Sure, with the pills my delusions come less frequently. But without my delusions, I feel awful. The depression and guilt are so much worse when you are alone. When you're not being tortured.

Sometimes it is better to suffer with fantasy than to be locked alone in reality.

"No." I tell her the truth, "I want to come off of them."

"Willow, you cannot come off of them."

I bite my lower lip nervously, and she picks up on it like a hawk.

"Are you still taking them, Willow? Please tell me you are still taking the medicine regularly."

My voice is small, and I don't bother lying, "No."

"How long have you not been taking them?" She scowls at me. The friendly smile on her face vanishes.

"Two weeks?" I tell her shakily. She hisses, and the sound echoes around the room, making me flinch.

"Willow, that's incredibly dangerous! You cannot come off medicine on your own terms. That is not safe. For you, for people around you..."

"I am not a danger to anyone!" I protest sharply.

"But you *could* be." My doctor tries desperately. I fall backwards in my seat and rock myself back and forth. *No*, I refuse to believe that I could be dangerous. My delusions never hurt anyone.

Unwillingly, I think back to the times where I've scratched at my own skin until I bled due to a delusion of smoke being stuck under my skin. Or the time where I had a scolding hot bath just to relive the torment of being in a fire-blazing house. Or the time I turned the oven on and then went to bed which caused the fucking fire...

*Shit.*

My jaw hardens. Perhaps the doctor is right.

She wheels her chair away from me and grabs another bottle of red pills. She pours two into her palm and thrusts it towards me. Shakily, I take them and reach for my water on the side. Under her intense gaze, I swallow the pills down.

"You must take these pills twice a day, Willow. They won't cure your delusions completely, but they should dull them. You can always take more if you have a particularly difficult day. Am I understood?" She asks me sternly. I nod my head slowly.

"I will be telling your brother about this too." She tuts.

"What! No! Please don't, Doctor. I promise I'll take them on time and regularly again." I hiss quickly. Guilt floods me. If Jake finds out I've been avoiding help, he'll be furious! All his money would be wasted.

She purses her lips and shakes her head at me sternly.

"No, Willow. This is a huge safeguarding issue." She scolds me. Weakly, I fall back in my chair and sulk. A tear slips down my face.

"Remind me," My therapist says, "What do we ask ourselves when we are struggling with what is real and what is not?"

A lump forms in my throat and I already feel my body tremble in anxiety. The world becomes a little darker. More normal. It hurts my eyes. I squint and shake my head.

"What?" I frown. Her words are like jelly. I can't seem to grab them as the world around me loses all hysteria. Everything becomes dull. Lonely. Revenge-free. And the guilt chokes me.

"What do we ask ourselves when we are struggling with what is real and what is not?" She repeats herself. The words stick in my head this time.

"Is anyone else reacting to the event? Is there any evidence that this is real? Am I feeling threatened?" I answer her. A sharp pain shoots through my finger. I peer down and stare as I subconsciously pull at the cuticles. It begins to bleed. Nervously, I wait for a delusion to kick in. Blood is one of my triggers. But nothing happens.

"Good." My doctor sighs in relief, "Now you just remember those, alongside your breathing skills and medication. You should be fine."

Numbly, I nod. She says that it will be fine. But I know for a fact, it won't be fine. *How can everything be fine when I'm still broken?* We are just throwing medicine at a lost cause.

# CHAPTER FIVE

## Mr Anderson's Pov:

T he low hum of my vehicle fills my ears. It pounds in and out of each ear drum and makes me cringe. Having said that, it's better than the sound of my racing heartbeat. Despite the September weather, it's surprisingly warm inside the car. I pull my jacket off and wipe the thin layer of sweat from my forehead. As I fall back into the car seat, I spot her. I spot the woman I've been waiting for.

Short, blonde locks bounce up and down as she strides towards the white building. She is wearing a dark grey power suit and clutching at a briefcase. Her face pulls into a permanent smug look. My fingers itch to smack it off her face.

I push the car into drive and slowly stalk closer towards the building she is walking towards.

As she disappears through the revolving doors at the front of the building, I slam on the breaks and jump out to follow her, leaving the engine still rumbling. Heart in my throat, I stagger up the three steps and collide with the glass door, tumbling inside.

However, the blonde woman is gone.

*Fuck, fuck, fuck!*

Frustratedly, I run my hands through my hair over and over to give my trembling fingers something to do. My heart hammers in my chest, causing sweat to pool at the back of my collar. To my left a receptionist glance's up from the desk to watch my nervous behaviour. When she smiles at me, hope blossoms in my chest.

"Hi," I hurry over to the small wooden desk she sits at and try to shoot her a winning smile. Although it's forced and feels wrong at a time like this, the woman melts under my gaze. "Sorry to interrupt, but what is this place please?"

At my strange question, she bristles slightly, shooting me a suspicious look.

"Excuse me?" She raises a thinly plucked eyebrow as she gives me a slow look up and down. I gulp.

"It's just that the sign outside has been blown over and…" I trail off into silence. My mind races and my heart thumps in my chest. *What could I say?* That*: "I am stalking the woman who ruined my life. I am waiting to find out which new man she is sleeping with today. I am looking for answers."*

"This is a doctor's office." The receptionist offers me a small smile which turns pitiful, "For mental health."

"Mental health?" I scoff, not caring about her reaction. I stumble backwards and look around myself again. Of course, Emily would come here. No doubt, she will be spinning her web of lies against me. Or worse, she will be sleeping with a therapist here. *I must find her.*

"Sir, are you okay?" The receptionist frowns, "Did you have an appointment?"

My head snaps back to her. *Did she think I was insane?* A scoff passes my lips. Perhaps I am fucking crazy. It's been six months since I last spoke to that bitch, and I'm still hung up on her every movement.

"No, but can you tell me if a lady called Emily Ande- Wait, no Emily Brownsky is here?" I kick myself when I try her married name. Emily would have stopped using my last name when we split up. She will most likely be using her maiden name until the divorce is finalised.

"Sir, I cannot tell you that, it is classified." Her lips pull into a grim line, and she reaches for the phone, "Is there anything else I can help you before you leave?"

I hold her a gaze menacingly for a little longer. My anger towards Emily is unmatched. I have never met a more bitter, hostile woman in my life. Her only aim in that miserable little life of hers is to ruin everybody else's. I just needed her to answer a couple questions and then I can move on with my life. And the bitch won't even give me that.

My knuckles turn white as I grip onto the reception desk. The receptionist hovers over the phone's keypad, silently threatening me with security. Her eyes hold more fear this time.

*Fuck, I am scaring her.*

I stumble backwards and throw my hands in the air. I can't be escorted from a mental health clinic! What if the university finds out? They'll get rid of me quicker than they hired me! And even then, they are most likely looking for a reason to get rid of me. I only just about got the job. Taking on a *'damaged'* student (in their words) sealed the deal.

"Sorry, sorry, I'll be going now." I shake my head bitterly, "Thank you for..."

*Nothing*, I want to say.

"Your time." I offer instead.

Before she can answer, I spin around on my feet and march back towards the door. However, I don't get far before I'm interrupted.

"Mr Anderson?" A small voice rings out to my right. With a flinch, I slowly turn to face where the noise came from, uneasiness settling in the pits of my stomach. The air catches in my throat at the sight of the girl.

*Willow.*

*What is she doing here?*

My eyebrows furrow together before I can stop them as I look at her up and down. She's wearing a long-sleeved grey turtleneck today; her dark hair hangs limply down her face, messy and tangled as if she uses her fingers, not a hairbrush. Her lips are turned downwards at the corners, as if she isn't pleased to see me; her skittish gaze refuses to stay in once place, darting between me, the floor, and over her shoulder to the receptionist I was just talking to.

"Willow." I breathe slowly. "What are you –"

I close my mouth sharply before I finish the sentence, realising how unprofessional it is. I *know* why she is here. The trauma, the therapy. The poor kid has a lot going on.

Clearing my throat, I stuff my sweaty hands into the back of my jeans pocket, trying to seem composed. My heart thuds in my chest so loud, there's a moment where I wonder if she can hear it.

"What are you doing here?" She asks shyly. At my shocked face, her eyes widen, and she shrinks further into her shoes. "If … if you want to tell me that is, no worries if you don't …"

I swallow hard. *How do I tell a student I am stalking my ex-wife in a mental hospital?*

I don't. Students love a drama, this would be the ultimate scoop, and then my teaching career would be ruined. With a final look at Willow, I jut my chin out, trying to look composed.

"Wrong building." I spit through gritted teeth. As soon as the words leave my mouth, I hate them. Willow recoils back as if I've punched her; she visibly flinches and crosses her arms over her chest, hugging herself tightly. Guilt swarms through my stomach as I spin on the ball of my feet and start my march towards the front door.

I shouldn't have snapped at Willow. She's a sensitive soul, and it's not her fault I'm in a foul mood at Emily.

However, I can't bring it in me to turn round and apologise. So, I storm away, into the car park. Despite my desperate attempts to end the conversation, Willow – to my surprise – calls after me and I hear the light thud of her footsteps as she chases me.

"Sir?" Her voice trembles as she speaks, and my body has a mind of its own when it turns to face her. *There they are.* Those wide, sad eyes. I purposefully focus on her button nose instead, unable to meet her gaze anymore. For the first time, I do not correct my name on her lips, and instead wait for her to continue her question.

She plays with her fingers nervously. "Have... have I done something to upset you?"

The question catches me off guard.

"What?" I gasp. Two metres in front of me, Willow shuffles nervously on the spot. Her eyes flicker to something besides us, but when I look, there's no one there. Slowly, I turn back to face her.

"Of course, you haven't upset me. Why would you think that?"

"I, uh." She scratches the back of her neck nervously, "We didn't get off to a great start and ever since then I feel like you're being hostile towards me."

*Brave.* She seems different today. More confident. And I can't help but wonder why. Is it because we are not in a classroom?

"You were late to my class." I tell her bitterly, trying to pull her back down to the meek, obedient student that I met in the lecture hall, "That is all. Forgive me if I am not polite to those who disrespect me and my time."

She looks shocked, mortified even, as she stumbles backwards. Her reaction forces me to rethink my words.

"I mean, I'm sorry you feel that way. It simply isn't true, however. There is no hostility between us." I tell her, "Perhaps you've been out of school for so long that you've forgotten academic professionalism. I'm like this with all my students."

*Low blow.* Her face drops and she winces. Now, she doesn't keep my gaze. She stares at the ground miserably.

"Oh." She says softly. She hugs herself and trembles. I scowl at her unusual behaviour, but I don't question it. She'll be gone in a couple months if she passes her exams. There is no point creating an academic bond between us. Or any bond for that matter. I can't have anyone growing too close otherwise they might know the real reason why I've moved to this town. The less they know, the better. I'll be gone soon, and I don't need anyone asking questions about that *mysterious professor.*

A honk of a car pulls me from my thoughts. I stare up at the old, rusty vehicle which drives towards us.

"I trust you will be on time to our next lecture?" I raise an eyebrow up at her. The words are bitter on my tongue, but I can't stop them. From in front of me, Willow doesn't respond. With a small nod of her head, she turns and creeps away. I watch her for a moment, before taking a deep shaky breath in. She walks as if there is glass beneath her feet, quickly shifting her weight on each foot, back stiff as if she can feel the shards ripping through her skin. I can't see her face, and for a moment, I'm thankful. Everybody experiences pain, and I don't need to think of Willow's any differently.

With one final look at her, I disappear back to my car. Off to my own miserable life where things are far worse than broken shards of glass beneath your toes.

# CHAPTER SIX

## Willow's Pov:

**M**iserably, I slump into the seat at the front of the lecture hall. This time, I have my pencil case and a piece of paper so that I do not need to interact with Mr Anderson. I don't know why he doesn't like me, but no matter his cheap excuses, I feel it deep in my bones. That man despises me. Perhaps he knows I'm crazy? Perhaps he judges me for my parents' death? He wouldn't be the first person to lash out on me because of it.

"Okay, today we will be working in pairs so find a partner." Mr Anderson announces to the class, eyeing up the masses of students who frantically look towards each other, trying to find someone to buddy up with. My heart sinks. I don't know anyone in the class, *how humiliating.*

As if on cue, I hear someone clearing their throat beside me.

"Want to pair up?"

My head snaps in the direction of the voice. A girl, not much older than me, sends me a dazzling smile as she takes a seat beside me. She's wearing an oversized black shirt with a skull and cross bones it, that drowns her petite frame. Her long legs are coated in black fishnet tights that catches the attention of every male in a ten-mile radius, and her jet-black hair is up, revealing hundreds of piercings in each ear. She's beautiful. I recognise her as the student who interrupted me and Mr Anderson earlier this week.

"Sure." I hear my voice respond, but it sounds far away, like it doesn't come from me. Nonetheless, the girl – *Olivia*, I think her name was- pulls her computer out of her bag, and shuffles in her seat to get comfortable. After a long moment, I offer her a shy smile.

"I'm Willow." I offer politely. Both her eyebrows shoot to the sky.

"Yes, I know." She scowls, "I've seen you around."

Humiliation coats my cheeks. *I was just trying to be nice.*

She smacks her lips as she blows a huge bubble of gum. Then her tongue pierces it, pulls it back into her mouth before she blows another bubble. The strawberry smell drifts between us.

"You will be working in pairs to discuss the first half of the book." Mr Anderson explains, pacing back and forth the stage of the lecture theatre.

As he paces, he tucks his hands behind his back, squaring his shoulders. Every footstep echoes out through the lecture hall, commanding attention. I try not to look, desperate not to attract his attention, *especially* after our last encounter.

From beside me, Olivia stretches out her long legs, and curses under her breath. To my surprise, she leans over, so close I can feel her breath on my neck.

"Have you read the book?" She whispers. The hairs on the back of my neck turn up at the feel of her warm breath on my face as I squirm in my seat. Her behaviour is abnormal and erratic. It makes my stomach churn. Crazy recognises crazy, but that doesn't mean I have to *welcome* crazy.

"No." I confess quietly, staying as polite as possible as if she is a wild beast ready to snap. "I didn't have time."

With a grin, Olivia sits back in her seat, blows a bubble again.

"Thank god." She smirks. "I haven't either."

From the front of the hall, Mr Anderson clicks a button on his laptop, which projects an image onto the interactive whiteboard. A long, large list of questions about the book appear, which he suggests should be a good starting point for discussion. As he reminds us to ask him questions if we get stuck, I can't help but feel his gaze flicker towards me.

My cheeks burn fiercely.

*Don't come over. Don't come over. Don't come over.* I plea wordlessly as everyone turns to their partners. Loud chatter floods the room as he instructs us to start our task. To my delight, in the corner of my eye I watch as Mr Anderson shoots us one long look, before taking a seat behind his desk, choosing not to approach.

*Finally, some good luck,* I think to myself wordlessly.

With a breath of relief, I turn to Olivia.

"So … What are we going to do about the questions?" I ask, just to start a conversation.

"Don't worry about them," She grins, flashing pearly white teeth. "I've resat this class like three times now. These questions don't appear on the test. They're just thinking questions. Thought provoking if you will."

"Yes, but we will need to answer them." I protest weakly. But with one raised eyebrow, Olivia silences me. The truth is I don't care to answer any questions today. I am exhausted. The pills make me feel like I'm slugging around with rocks in my shoes. Each movement feels heavy.

"So why do you have extra sessions with Sir?" Olivia asks abruptly. The question takes me by surprise, and I have to steal myself a couple of erratic heartbeats to come up with an answer. However, she doesn't rush me. With a steady, reassuring smile, she continues to blow bubbles in her gum and waits patiently for an answer.

"I missed the summer term of school last year, so I'm making up for it through extra classes." I explain warily. Olivia frowns at me, "Why did you miss school?"

This makes me freeze. *Does she not know? Is she the only person in this town who hasn't read about the awful tragedy of the house fire? Does she keep her head in the sand or something?*

"My parents died." I give her the easy answer. She blows out a breath.

"That sucks." She says before popping her gum. She has a complete disregard for the topic. Instead of the usual pitiful glances and pinched lips, she tilts back in her seat, picking at the dirt under her nails as if we are discussing what to eat for dinner later.

"But at least you're back now." She offers with a small smile. I nod my head. But inside I am mortified.

"You didn't miss much." She continues talking, "Just a load of bullshit and crappy questions on the exams."

"Is that why you've resat so many times? Are the exams difficult?" I say before a mortified expression stains my face, "Oh my goodness, that was so rude of me. I, I er, I didn't mean it!"

As if I had just told the funniest joke, Olivia's head snaps backward and she snorts through fits of laughter. My cheeks burn brighter than they ever have before, and I keep my head low to avoid the curious gazes of the students around us. She doesn't stop laughing and the humiliation eats up at me.

"Why was that funny?" I frown, not getting the joke. If she is going to mock me for simple questions perhaps, I am better working alone. The bitterness floods through me.

"No, you're right. I'm just not good at exams I guess." She says, still with a smile on her dark lips. The pitch in her voice tells me she is lying.

"Is that why you came to see the professor last week?" I raise an eyebrow, "Are you getting extra tuition too?"

"Sure." She answers. Again, she blows her bubble gum out. I take this as a clear indication not to push any further. My gaze shoots to the board to start on the questions, however there is a body blocking the view. Leaning over us, and with the tips of his ears red, Mr Anderson jerks a bin under Olivia's nose.

"Gum. Bin. Now." He grunts. The sound makes me shiver, not used to hearing such an authoritative tone. However, Olivia doesn't seem to react.

Slowly, she cocks her head to the side, biting her lower lip as she maintains eye contact. My heart is drumming so loudly in my ears at Mr Anderson's close presence that I can't hear the quiet words they are exchanging. But it feels tense and heated. Finally, Olivia rocks forwards in her chair, and spits the gum into the bin. It smacks the inside wall with a light thud, much to her delight. Then, she slowly pulls back, never taking her eyes off the professor.

Mr Anderson's lip twitches slightly but he doesn't fight back. He chooses his battle wisely.

"How are we getting on with the questions?" He asks, directing the conversation away, and with it, his gaze. It lands on me. My blood goes cold.

"Erm …" I falter over my words before resorting to silence. The idea of admitting I haven't done the work makes my heart squeeze tightly. This man already hates me, how will he react to this?

Luckily, Olivia swoops into the rescue.

"We are on question four." She lies with a sweet smile. In my chest, my heart is like a hammer, and I subtly wipe my sweaty palms on my jeans.

Mr Anderson looks slowly between us – her with her innocent smile, and me looking incredibly guilty – and then down to our empty pieces of paper.

"Oh really?" He grits out. "Where are your answers?"

"In our heads. We are discussing them all first before we make notes." Once again, Olivia lies easily, like she's done it a thousand times. Flinching, I glance up at Mr Anderson, curious to see if he's buying her lies.

*Bad decision.*

His piercing coal-coloured eyes meet mine. Time freezes.

For the longest of time, we stare at each other as I hold my breath, desperately hoping he can't hear my thoughts. He arches an eyebrow and scans my face. I feel like a scolded child, and he almost takes pride in it. A slight twitch on his lips has me sinking further into my seat, begging it to swallow me whole.

When Olivia clears her throat slightly, he finally breaks eye contact, turning his gaze back to her.

"I thought you wanted to pass these exams." He says coldly. "Lying will not help you." Then he glares at me, "As for you. I will see you after class and you can explain to me why you didn't attend yesterday's lesson or tuition session. Oh, *and* why you haven't completed any work today."

Humiliation creeps through me as my cheeks stain bright red. Every part of me is on edge, a nervous wreck under his steady, calm stare. Just as I think I'm going to be sick from the silence that is torturing me, he speaks again.

"I suggest that you both start reading the designated chapters immediately and catch up on the questions later." He commands. My mouth feels so dry that I know I can't form any words. Instead, I nod feverishly, keeping my gaze low, unable to look at the disappointment in his face. I hear him leave with a grunt, and try to relax my tensed muscles, but it's incredibly difficult.

As if sensing my discomfort, Olivia bumps shoulders with me.

"Don't sweat it, he's all bark and no bite." She offers gently. "He'll calm down by the time class is up."

Tears are swimming in my eyes no matter how hard I try to blink them away. I am exhausted, both mentally and physically. The idea of reading a stupid fucking book is the last thing on my mind.

"Here." Olivia says before scribbling something down on a piece of paper. She pushes it towards me, and I stare at the list of numbers.

"That's my number." She says, "Message me if you want to revise together or even just hang out."

I scowl down at the piece of paper in confusion. Olivia hadn't exactly been the friendliest to me so far, and now she is inviting me to hang out. My head thumps as I tried to piece it together.

"Oh, and there is a party this weekend. You should come." She offers, "I mean, it will do you good to get you out of that house. To actually live a little."

The breath in my chest is stolen from me. I want to flee and never talk to her again. Lately, I've been having a very hard time not self-sabotaging. I want to push everybody away from me and ignore the whole world. I am unworthy of happiness. I killed my parents. But then I know exactly what Jake would say if I rejected this offer. He'd kill me for purposely isolating myself. Doctor Jane too.

"Thanks." I say with a small smile, tucking the paper into my pocket.

"No probs." She shrugs, before turning her attention away from me.

The paper in my pocket feels heavy. Feels wrong. But it's a distraction from Mr Anderson's intense gaze. I sigh as I add buying a phone to my to do list for the day. I have never needed one up until now. The only person I talk to is Jake and he always knows where to find me. *In bed, struggling to sleep.*

Perhaps the future for Willow Langly is looking a little brighter.

* * *

**MR ANDERSON'S POV:**

The bell echoes around the lecture hall. For the last five minutes, the students have been slowly packing up. They switch off ten minutes towards the end of class- I'm not stupid. I see the way the sparkle fades and exhaustion takes a hold of them.

My eyes catch Willow as she frantically tidies up. With an amused smirk on my lips, I watch as she tries to escape in the mass of students all leaving the room.

"Miss Langly!" I boom. She freezes on the spot, clutching her bag against her chest. Slowly, she turns to face me, and a sheepish look covers her face.

"And where do you think you're going?" I try to hide my amusement with a frown. Opening and closing her mouth, Willow struggles for a response. To my dismay, it's Olivia once more who comes to her rescue.

"Oh, sorry Sir! Willow and I have an afterschool club that we were going to go to –" My disobedient student lies. I steal a moment to shoot her a dark look. Whether Olivia knows this or not, but she has a nervous tic that she does every time she lies – her left eyebrow twitches and she blinks in rapid succession. Here she is now, twitching and blinking.

With a big sigh, I rub my face tiredly, before turning to Willow, knowing the lesser evil of the two to battle.

"Running away from this conversation won't solve anything." I tell her sternly. "I would have just found you again to continue the conservation."

A small shiver wracks through her body at my words, and it makes me cringe. I sound like a crazy stalker. *I am,* I add bitterly in my head. As if she can read my mind, her gaze flickers quickly between me and the floor. I hastily change the subject to avoid the awkward tension in the room.

"Why didn't you read 'One who flew over the cuckoo's nest' over the weekend?" I ask her. Her cheeks tinge a beautiful red colour.

"I slept through the day. *Days.*" She confesses. My eyebrows burrow together, "Are you telling me that you slept forty-eight hours and that is why you didn't do your homework?"

She bites her lower lip again and nods her head quickly. I frown. She must be lying. That isn't possible. And yet I don't know why she would lie about that; it's such an odd excuse. It's too precise.

"Okay." I release a sigh, "You need to try and keep up. You're already at a disadvantage with how much you have to learn on top of your final year work."

"Yes, Mr Anderson." She says quietly. It sends shivers through me.

"Take a seat." I tell her and she quickly jumps into action. She slings her bag down on the desk and pulls out the books. As she is doing that, I pull a chair in front of the small desk and take a seat. Out of the corner of my eye, I watch Olivia slowly creeping out of the room, not wanting to be lectured as well. I pretend not to notice her as I hear the door slide shut with a soft *click*. Around us, the room is empty, a drastic change to five minutes ago.

"So, we have three months until your exams." I begin, "Do you have your copy of 1984 to hand? Let's revise last year's material today. You should have finished reading that text."

Another sheepish look crosses her face. She hesitates before reaching into the bag. Slowly, she pulls out a broken looking book. The front cover is missing, and the pages are all bent.

"I got it from a charity shop." She confesses. Slowly, I nod in understanding. I look between her broken copy and my pristine one. Something in me itches to swap copies. To let her have something of value.

"Okay." I remain professional, "Let's start reading."

I flick to the right page before instructing her to do the same. As per my instructions, she begins reading. My eyes remain on the words on the page, but I am swooned by her soft voice. It holds such misery and cracks regularly. It's as if she has only just learnt to speak again.

Her finger teases the corner of the page before turning it over. I am hooked by her little mannerisms. The way she scrunches her nose when she struggles on a word, how she twiddles with her hair, wrapping it around one slim finger before curling it on another finger. She makes beautiful patterns with those dark tendrils.

"Of pain you could wish only one thing: that it should stop. Nothing in the world was so bad as physical pain. In the face of pain there are no heroes." She reads the quote out loud, but it seems to bring her own type of agony. She gulps and pauses momentarily. I would pay great money to know what she is thinking right now. Her face contorts into many different expressions, but they are each inscrutable. *What is she thinking?*

My own body responds to the quote. Orwell couldn't be more wrong. Physical pain was awful, yes. But there is nothing quite like mental torture. The waves of agony, repeating again and again until you want to rip your hair out and run away. My mind flickers back to my wife and all the shit she put me through. The endless affairs, the mental abuse, the gaslighting, backstabbing, disloyalty...

"Sir?" Willow's voice pulls me from my thoughts. I quickly regain control of my expressions and release the pages from my harsh grip.

"It's Mr. Anderson." I grunt, using anger to hide my thoughts. She doesn't answer me, but she also doesn't resume reading, so I take the opportunity to quiz her.

"Do you agree?" I ask her, "Do you agree with Orwell, that physical pain is the worst thing possible?"

"No." She answers quickly, "No, I do not agree."

I offer her silence to see if she wishes to expand on her answer. But she doesn't. She keeps her cards close to her chest, never offering any more information than she has to. We are very alike in that regard. I don't push for an answer, so I change subject.

"Read page 231 again and tell me what stands out. Which quote would you analyse in the exam?" I instruct. She frowns and thumbs through the pages. Her lips part nervously as she frantically tries to find the correct page. I spot the slight tremble in her body and her flushed cheeks.

"Here." I tell her, reaching out for the book. However, just as I go to take it, I accidentally brush past her hands. The touch is magnetising. The air in my lungs vanishes and I feel my body grow rigid. As if she feels the connection too, Willow gasps and pulls her hands away. The lack of touch makes me feel empty. I want to restore my fingers on her smaller hands. But I resist. I *must* be professional.

She blinks rapidly before thrusting the book up to her face. She scans the page for a quote, for a distraction. I force myself to take some steadying breaths.

"This one." She says almost breathlessly, "Under the spreading chestnut tree, I sold you and you sold me: There lie they, and here lie we, under the spreading chestnut tree."

I rock back in the chair and look at her thoughtfully,

"Why that quote?"

"Well, it's a quote on the song about the place where lovers and rebels go to meet. And at the end, the two main characters really do sell each other out to the leading Party; it's ironic and foreshadowing a bad end." She whispers, looking at the words on the page with a sad smile, "It's hard to imagine the person you love selling you out."

I jolt. Whether she meant for me to hear that last part or not, I am not sure. But her analysis makes me wince. It's like an elastic band around my heart. I know all too well what it feels like to have a loved one sell you out. To use and dispose of you at their convenience.

"Sorry, did I say something wrong?" She gawps at me in shock. I shake my head quickly.

"No, no, no." I splutter, "Beautiful quote. Well done."

Eventually, my eyes meet hers again. She watches me intensely as if she's searching for more. I feel myself subconsciously move towards her. I shuffle forward in the chair. Her lips part and an inscrutable look dances in her dark eyes. My fingers itch to touch her soft cheek. To run a thumb down her face, down her neck, towards her breasts, and then back to her lips. *What would they taste like?* Despair, probably. My favourite.

*Fuck! No, Liam, no!*

Startled, I pull backwards and shake my head. To put more distance between us, I shuffle backward in the chair and reach for my water bottle, frantically gulping down the cold water to clear my head. I must stop these thoughts. What am I thinking? As far as she is concerned, she is my student, for at least another three months until she passes her exams. Or even less if I can find that slippery bitch of an ex-wife quickly. I can't risk this job. My revenge.

"Turn to page one hundred and four. Write me an essay on how Orwell presents the main character as a depressing hero." I spit out a task. Anything to get those gorgeous eyes off me. A look of confusion flickers across her face before she stares down at the blank paper in front of her. I look at those rosy cheeks and long lashes which flutter around as she looks between me and the paper.

I take a deep breath and force the thoughts away. Willow Langly is my student, not my plaything. And I will not combine the two, no matter how much I want to.

# CHAPTER SEVEN

## Willow Pov:

"Go on, I'll get you in an hour." Jake tells me as he parks the car. My body feels heavy as I look at the depressingly clinical therapy building.

"You don't want to be late, come on." Jake presses gently. I grab my water bottle from the side before leaning in to give him a side embrace.

"I'll see you in a bit?" I smile up at him weakly. He nods his head before stretching over to open the car door for me.

"Yes, and we can go for dinner if you'd like?" He beams.

"What?" I frown, "We don't have the money."

A long silence pools between us and Jake's smile grows.

"I was going to tell you later, but you look as if you could do with some cheering up." He smirks, "I got a promotion!"

"Oh, Jake!" I blurt, "That's amazing! Congratulations! I knew you could do it!"

A blush coats his cheeks and shrugs his shoulders like it's nothing, "It's not much more, but it's definitely a start. So, where would you like to eat this evening? My treat."

I lick my lips hungrily as my stomach growls. I could eat anything right now.

"Toby Carvery?" My brother raises an eyebrow. I nod my head frantically. Dad used to take us there all the time as children when my Mum was working. He couldn't cook for the life of him, so he had to buy us food if we were to avoid starvation.

"Sounds great." I agree before jumping out the car, "Thanks Jake. I will see you in an hour."

He sends me a wink as I slam the car door shut. With a newfound happiness, I almost skip into the building to get it over and done with. I push the doors open but stumble to a halt as I turn down a corridor towards Doctor Jane's office.

A blonde-haired woman bends over, clutching her chest. She pants as she tries to catch her breath. One hand clutches her enormous pregnant belly and the other splays itself against the wall to help maintain her balance.

"Are you okay?" I whisper as I walk past her. Her face is pulled together in pain, and she sounds like she is struggling. When she hears me, she masks her discomfort and lets out a shaky laugh.

"Y-Yeah," She stumbles on her words as she tries to steady her breathing, "Do you mind?"

She reaches out for my water bottle. I quickly oblige and let her have some of the water. I wasn't going to drink it all anyways. She gulps some of it down before screwing the lid back on.

"Thanks," She says with a polite smile, "I had to run here and it's exhausting, especially whilst being pregnant."

"Are you allowed to run whilst pregnant?" I hear my naïve words escape before I could stop them. She shrugs at me and smiles, "We will find out."

I scowl at her cryptic words but quickly push them away.

"Anyways," She says, handing me my water back, "Thank you for this."

And with that, she waddles away into another room. I think nothing of it as I slide into Doctor Jane's office. She greets me with a wide smile.

"Willow!" She says happily, pointing a hand towards my usual seat. I take it quickly, excited to get this session over and done with.

"How has your week been?" She smiles.

*Good. I am going to Toby Carvery after this,* I want to boast, but it's a bit of a niche thing. Doctor Jane looks as if she has the money to go there every day. And then my mind flickers back to University. To Mr Anderson. The happiness turns to nervousness. I had so desperately wanted to kiss him yesterday. I might have dreamt the way he looked at me, but something in my stomach twisted and urged me to shuffle closer.

"Good." I tell her confidently. For a second, she seems taken aback by my enthusiasm but quickly masks it. I take a sip of my water to wet my dry mouth. Doctor Jane engages in further polite conversation about my week. *How is school? How is Jake? Have you made any friends?*

I tell her all about Jake's promotion and Olivia giving me her number. Time seems to slip by quickly. Then a bitter smell floats around the room. I stare down and spot a cigarette in my fingers.

"When…" I start to question but I stop myself.

This is the trick with therapy. You go to get better, and yet you have to hide the truth or else you're sent away to the loony bin. I am one wrong move away from wearing grippy socks for the rest of my life.

My lips part as I stare down at the small trail of smoke which seeps from my cigarette. The tendrils dance around and create patterns. First, a rough outline of a dog and then two people. *My parents.* They dance around together in the smoke, performing a dance to an unheard song. My heart leaps in my chest. Dad spins Mum around on the dancefloor and it's almost as if I can hear their laughter. Growing up, my parents used to take up the whole living room to dance together. It was their bonding time. Sometimes, I would sneak onto the stairs to watch them through the banisters. They thought I was in bed, asleep, but in reality, I was enjoying their happiness. The happiness which died shortly after my eighteenth birthday due to his affair. I shake my head and the smoke figures disappear.

"We need to talk about that night." My therapist tries again. But my voice is gone. Slowly, I bring the cigarette to my lips to take a puff. I need the relief. I follow it with a huge gulp of my cold water.

"I really don't want to." I say quietly. Doctor Jane doesn't answer so I peer up at her quizzically. I expect her to protest, to grow mad at me for being so unresponsive. However, my eyes are not on her.

My mother has returned. She stands behind Doctor Jane, arms crossed over her chest. I can feel the anger sifting around the room. Her whole body is alight in flames and even though she is on the other side of the room, I can feel the heat licking at my body. A layer of sweat coats my forehead.

"Those pills." I whisper to my Doctor without ever removing my eyes from my Mother, "I don't think they work."

"No?" My Doctor raises an eyebrow, "Perhaps we should consider upping the dosage."

My head nods frantically. The anger from my mother oozes into the room and crawls into my heart. It squeezes it until I choke on the anxiety.

"Tell me." Doctor Jane presses, "Tell me what happened that night. We will make no progress until you stop being in denial about the event. We can't keep you drugged up forever, Willow. I can increase the dosage now, but you must open up."

"But!" I protest, staring into my mother's furious eyes. They are balls of pure white and yet I can feel her gaze locked firmly onto me.

"Another reason for these delusions will be guilt, Willow. Speaking about that night might help you work through some of these feelings." She presses.

My mother cocks her head to the side. I can't tell if she is threatening me to talk, or to stay quiet. My whole-body trembles in fear. It feels as though my psychosis is growing worse. Never before has my Mother haunted me during the day. She reserved that luxury for the night. And yet recently she is always here. Always watching.

"Well, I was hungry, so I went downstairs to make dinner." I begin the story though my voice cracks in fear.

"Go on." My doctor gently pushes.

A tear slips down my face as my mother takes another step towards me. Only now that she's stepped away from her smoke cloud which covered below her hips I can see her outfit. She wears the clothes she wore that night. A long, leopard print skirt, with a long-sleeved black shirt. She looked so pretty that night. One minute, she was practicing a dance with my father with her beautiful long lashes and perfect round lips, and the next, she was being wheeled out on a stretcher, skin bubbled away and bone protruding out of the holes.

A lump in my throat forms.

"I turned the oven on and made myself a cup of tea. Then I left the room to go and get the fishfingers from the freezer which was out back." I explain. My bottom lip wobbles. Doctor Jane leans forward in her seat expectantly. She knows exactly what happened that night. Everybody in the town has read my witness report. But everybody enjoys a first-hand recount. It's like a real-life soap story.

"I put the fishfingers on the side and took my tea upstairs. I was just putting the tea in my room, so I didn't have to juggle carrying that as well as my food when it was ready." I justify my actions defensively, "But I got distracted and finished my tea upstairs whilst I waited for the food to cook."

The silence drifts around the room. My mother's eyes are wide as she listens to my story intently. There is still an intense feeling drifting around the room, but I desperately try to block it out.

"And then what?" Doctor Jane frowns at me. I purse my lips and look down at my twiddling fingers.

"And then I can't remember." I whisper guiltily, "They said I fell asleep. That the oven exploded and started the fire."

"When did you wake up?" My doctor shakes her head slightly. I've heard it all before from the police officers. My story doesn't add up. I know it doesn't. But it is the truth. I would never kill my own parents, and they knew this too. They had no motive to pin me down with, so it was ruled to be an accident. *Because it was a fucking accident.*

"I am not sure." I tell her weakly, "I just remember waking up outside in the bushes. Someone shook me awake."

My mother disappears now. She no longer watches me intently, with that awful look. Now that she is gone, the breath slowly comes back into my lungs.

"So, you jumped? From your window?" Doctor Jane presses. I shrug my shoulders, "That's what they say. You have to believe me, Doctor, I have no recollection of that night."

"And you were taking your meds regularly back then, right?" She raises an eyebrow.

"Is this an interrogation?" I spit, suddenly very defensive. I shuffle around in my seat and pull my legs to my chest. My doctor winces and pulls back quickly.

"No, of course not, Willow. I am just trying to understand what happened so we can help you more." She justifies but it's futile. I don't know her angle, but it surely isn't to help me. My best bet is that she's trying to get a confession. I wonder how much money the police have paid her to damn the crazy woman.

"Don't let your paranoia take over." She tells me sternly. I shake my head. 'Paranoia' is the term they use when they want to dismiss your fucking feelings. I stumble to my feet and head towards the window.

"Willow, where are you going?" She frowns, a little pitched in her tone.

"To look at the fucking squirrels." I bark, forcing the blinds open. I need a distraction. I need air. My fingers fumble at the lock but I don't get far. Doctor Jane leaps in front of me.

"Willow!" She shrieks, "What are you doing?"

"I just need to open the…" I begin but the world seems to become hazy.

"The, the, the." I stumble over my words as my head becomes heavy. My fingers grab the window ledge as I try to steady myself.

"Code red!" Doctor Jane shrieks to nobody. I peer around, trying to figure out what's going on, but my body is suddenly being touched by strangers. Weakly, I resist but hands grab my arms and lower me to the ground. My face presses against the scratchy carpet and the world hums into a dull silence around me. The last thing I see before blacking out is my lit cigarette, laying on the carpet in front of me.

# CHAPTER EIGHT

## Mr Anderson's Pov:

The class falls quiet as I enter the room. Dozens of blank faces stare back at me, all waiting for today's two-hour long lecture. I can see the boredom already floating around the room. Nobody wants to be here. They can get the materials online from the comfort of their bedrooms, and yet they must be here to get attendance marks. Without attendance, you are not allowed to sit your end of year exams to progress into the next year.

Slowly, I scan the audience before checking my watch. The time is ten past eleven. *Where is Willow? Will she be late again? Did she not learn her lesson last time?* Somebody clears their throat at the front of the room, pulling me back into reality.

"Okay, here are your questions." I declare, heading towards my laptop and pulling up the PowerPoint. Twenty questions appear on screen.

"You all should have read the last three chapters before this session. Here are some plenary questions to see how well you understood it." I instruct them, "We will go through it in the second hour."

The class hums as the students begin working together.

Miserably, I fall back into my seat. *What if Willow is purposely ignoring my class because of Monday's session?* I was too close to kissing her. It was unprofessional. Sure, she might be twenty-two and a consenting adult, but I still hold some duty of care towards her as her professor.

That is until I find Emily and can leave this town.

I move the mouse on my computer and split the screen so that my slide with all the questions doesn't leave the massive projector screen at the front of the class. Then I slide my mouse over to safari. Letter by letter, I spell out Gmail before clicking on the tab. It takes me a while because my thumb no longer bends to reach the bottom keys on the keyboard. I push my thoughts away from my thumb.

My emails pop up. I scroll down them, looking for something to do for an hour.

My attention is caught instantly. Doctor Jane has messaged me. I double click on the email which doesn't have a subject. My eyes skim over the email.

*"Dear Mr Anderson,*

*This is an update on your tutee Willow Langly.*

*Firstly, how often are you having sessions with her? I would like reports on the tuition please so I can get more funding from the University. She doesn't like to discuss school during therapy so it would be great if you could give me an update at least once a week.*

*Secondly, and more significantly, Willow poses a huge threat to herself. During Tuesday's therapy session, Willow tried to jump out of the window. She presented symptoms of hysteria, paranoia, and delusions. This ultimately led her to be reckless. As a result, she must stay home for a day or two, and take a higher dose of her prescribed medicine.*

*Due to this, she might fall behind on class this week. My recommendation is home visits and continuing tuition from the comfort of her own home. Check the welcome email I sent you at the beginning of term for her address and contact details.*

*If this is something you are unable to do, please let me know and we can work something out.*

*Speak soon,*

*Doctor Jane Dowding."*

My heart pounds in my chest and the sweat licks at my body. Mortified, I reread the email over and over until the words physically make me feel sick.

"Fuck." I growl under my breath. *Why would she try to take her own life? What happened? Was it me? Did I scare her too much?* My breath is snatched at the last thought. *Fuck*! I knew I had to be professional! *And now I will have to do house visits? Is that such a good idea?*

No. *Yes!* No.

I throw myself to my feet and all the eyes tear around to me.

"Finish the questions at home. I will send out the answers later this evening." I bark before fleeing the room. There are some protests as they quickly pack up their things. I don't even care for the flood of complaints from the nerdier students amongst them. Right now, my attention is fixed on Willow.

I don't think I've ever run quicker to my car. My working thumb frantically scrolls down my emails until I find the welcome email. *32 Crescent Drive,* I read the address out loud as I plug it into google maps. *A ten-minute drive.*

I throw the car into drive and speed off out of the campus carpark. My heart races in my chest and it feels as if there is an elastic band around it. Why am I so worried about her? She is my student. Nothing more, nothing less. And yet I have a strange sort of possessive pull towards her. Maybe its guilt?

Unwillingly, I think back to my wife. I used to be attracted to her in the way my body seems to respond to Willow. Emily would pull you close by the tie and just hold you there. Her piercing, crystal eyes would bear into your own for what felt like hours. She is my drug. *Was* my drug. Whatever Emily said, went. Perhaps it will be the same with Willow?

Pressed up against the wall, Emily would hold you there, trembling in anticipation. She enjoyed your anxiety as she slowly brought her lips to your ear. Then, she would pause. The silence would be unbearable, and you wanted to snap, to let the beast out. But boy was she a brilliant tamer. After a long while, she'd whisper dirty promises into your ear. My Emily would have you on your knees before you knew it.

Perhaps that is why my wife made such a good mistress to the other men. A lump in my throat forms as I think back to all the men she snuck into my house. Into my bed. And all the times she'd flee the house to go to '*work*', only for me to follow her and find her in the arms of another man.

Obviously, I'd protest and start an argument. I would pack my bags and arrange for a place to stay for the night. But my little Emily had a way with words. If I didn't know any better, I'd say she was Aphrodite incarnate. The seductress would keep you on your knees, submissive, loyal, all the while she spread her legs for anything that moved. She got off on my pain. My misery. And I was trapped.

"Fuck!" I growl as I speed up. Emily is in the past. Well, almost. I just needed to find out *why. Why did she leave me six months ago? What changed? Had she finally given me mercy by breaking the spell between us? Did she find someone better?*

The last thought makes my blood boil. I hate her, I fucking hate her and yet I am infatuated. There is a curse running through my blood. I love too hard. Too violently.

A dingy little block of flats appears into view as I turn the corner. They look like they haven't been painted in decades with its peeling plaster and eggshell coloured paint in random splodges. In some flats, windows are missing and have been replaced with carboard. Out front, the bins pile up and it causes quite a stench.

I lift my shirt up to my nose and get out of the car. After double checking the number of her flat, I race up the stairs. They make strange dinging noises as I put my weight on them, and they shake in the wind. My grip on the banister tightens. I wouldn't be surprised if the rusty thing gives way.

Finally, I arrive outside a dark door with a thirty-two on it. The number has been scribbled on the door in some sort of whiteboard marker, and it is slightly smudged. I turn my nose up at the disgusting block of flats. I cannot believe anyone lives here. Let alone timid little Willow.

Before I can change my mind, I knock on the door. However, under my touch, the door opens. *It is unlocked*! I frown at the complete lack of security. She lives in the roughest part of the town and still keeps her front door unlocked.

"Hello?" I call out but I get no response. It smells of lavender in here, a stark contrast to the rubbish tips outside. Nervously, I take a step in. The welcome mat is a bit of cut up carpet. It sticks to the bottom of my shoes. I lunge over it and look around.

On my left, there is an ajar door. A basic kitchen stares back at me. There isn't even have a kettle nor microwave but there is a pot of hot water on the stove. In the same room, a worn-down sofa. It looks second hand with the scratch marks on it. It is clear she has tried to make it look more appealing by throwing a soft looking blanket on it and a couple of red pillows, but it is hard to cover the discolouration. The room is empty.

"Hello?" I try again, "Willow?"

Again, there is no response. My palms become sweaty as I open the door on the right. It is a basic bedroom with a single bed in one corner and a wardrobe in the other. The bed has been made and the room looks fairly tidy. Something tells me this isn't Willow's room.

I take a step backwards and peer down the hallway. One final door watches me.

Everything in me screams to turn around and leave the house, but I can't. My curiosity gets the better of me and my legs move me automatically toward the closed door, where the lavender smell increases. With a gulp, I knock gently on the rotting oak door.

A long pause stretches out.

Finally, I brave it and slowly push the door open.

This room is in stark difference to the other room. Clothes are everywhere, and there are boxes with empty glasses of water stacked on top of them. My eyes shoot to the bed where a figure lays. Even though she is facing away from me, with the covers pulled up to her neck, I instantly recognise her. I pause and debate whether I should wake her up.

On the one hand, she still has University work to do. On the other, she has had a crazy week. She might not want to see me right now.

Suddenly, she moves; she tosses and turns. A low cry leaves her lips, and her hands shoot out to her neck. It's as if she is trying to pry off someone strangling her. Mortified, I watch wide eyed as she starts to choke and splutter.

"Willow?" I call out nervously before trying again more sternly, "Willow! Wake up!"

I charge over, something primal taking a hold of me. It hurts to watch her in pain. Suddenly, she shoots up in bed. Her shoulders rise and fall quickly as she desperately tries to catch her breath.

"It's okay, I'm here." I tell her, "Are you okay?"

Without warning, she throws herself into my arms. A small whimper falls past her lips. Momentarily, I freeze up. I shouldn't be consoling her, nor touching her. It goes completely against protocol. But as she quietly sobs in my arms, I can't help but pull her closer. My other hand gently strokes her hair, and it seems to soothe her.

"What happened?" I whisper. A long string of hiccups fall from her lips before she pulls back. Her face is all red and sweaty. She wipes her tears away with her pyjama sleeve.

"How did you get in?" She changes the subject.

In the dim light of the room, her puffy eyes dart between me and her bedroom door suspiciously. However, she looks too tired to be upset. I swallow the lump in my throat as I sheepishly rub the back of my neck.

"The door was unlocked." I say nervously. Perhaps it was wrong of me to let myself in. But at the same time, I don't care. I awoke her from whatever awful dream she was having. Personally, I know how awful it is to be trapped in a nightmare. My whole fucking marriage was like it.

"What were you dreaming about?" I frown. Uncomfortably, she shuffles backwards and pulls her legs to her chest before hugging them tightly. Another hiccup falls from her lips.

"My mum." She whimpers. I cock my head to the side as I watch her try and be strong.

"She was strangling me." She confesses before pushing herself off the bed. She heads over to a carboard box and pulls out a bottle of pills. Swiftly, she pours two into her hands.

"What are those?" I frown, grabbing at her hand. Mortified, she looks at me and the pills.

"They help me." She whispers.

"With what?" I scowl, pulling at the bottle. I read the label, but the name of the pill is unrecognisable. Her therapist told me she suffered with anxiety and depression, and yet these pills look nothing like usual antidepressants.

"Distinguishing reality and fiction." She mutters before pulling the bottle back out of my hands. With a sigh, she pours the pills back into the pot before sitting back on the bed.

"I struggle with delusions." She confesses sadly, staring at the floor. I shuffle closer to her, sensing she needs comforting.

"What kind of delusions?" I gently probe. She releases a long sigh before turning to face me.

"It doesn't matter." She shakes her head, "Why are you here?"

I am taken aback with her sudden abruptness, but I don't show it.

"Doctor Jane told me you tried to take your own life yesterday. I'm here to check if you're okay." I tell her. Her jaw slackens and she looks at me with wide eyes.

"I didn't try to take my own life." She hisses, throwing herself to her feet. A sudden fit of rage seems to take hold of her.

"Why is she telling everybody that!" She cries out, chucking her arms around, "I just wanted to open the fucking window! Is that *so* hard to understand?"

I remain quiet, watching as she explodes. Timid little Willow seems to have a short fuse. With an impressed smile, I listen quietly.

"First, they accuse me of burning my fucking house down and jumping from that window, and now they say I'm trying to kill myself on a random Tuesday evening! Why are they lying?" A solitary tear slips down her face, "What do they have to gain with accusing me of murder and suicide?"

The smile is snatched from my lips. Blankly, I watch as she paces around the room. I have never seen her this agitated and wound up. Everything I've learnt about her points to craziness. And yet as she stands here, telling me her side to the story, I can't help but believe her.

"I trust you." I tell her quietly. The crazed look across her face vanishes as she turns to stare at me in disbelief.

"W-what? You do?" She frowns, in shock.

"Yes." I answer simply, "I don't believe you tried to kill yourself yesterday."

"But you don't know me." She scowls at me before pursing her lips. I shrug my shoulders, "And yet something tells me you are innocent."

Warily, she watches me with wide eyes. A whole host of emotions flicker across her face.

"Good." She answers after a long pause. Finally, she takes her place on the bed next to me.

"Good." I repeat.

A small flicker of a smile covers her lips. Her eyes dart between my face and her fingers in her lap.

"Thank you for coming to check on me I guess." She whispers. I shrug it off.

"Doctor Jane told me I had to do a home visit to keep you caught up on the work."

"Oh." She seems almost disappointed in my answer. Before I can stop myself, I lay a hand on hers reassuringly. The touch takes my breath away and I feel dizzy. A look of longing dances in her dark eyes as she stares up at me. It takes everything within me to hold back. I could lose my job over this. It is wrong. It is forbidden. And yet it feels so fucking right.

Slowly, she leans in. I can feel her warm breath against my face and smell the sweetness of her strawberry shampoo and conditioner which I smelt on our first encounter. It swarms my senses and makes me feel drunk. Subconsciously, I raise my hand to her face. She presses further into my touch as I run my thumb up and down her cheek. Her skin is so soft. So warm.

Her eyes are locked on my lips as she inches closer and closer towards me. Then her eyes flutter shut, and I hear her breathing grow more erratic. This sends me over the edge. Without thinking, I press my lips against hers and kiss her passionately. A small moan escapes her lips. Quickly, she raises herself to her knees and deepens the kiss. My hands jump to her lower back to try and steady her but something primal has taken over her body. She readjusts her position until she is sitting on my lap with her fingers latched in my hair. Desperately, I respond to her passionate pace. The taste of her is like no other woman I have ever tasted. It's a dangerous, forbidden type of lust. It makes it that much stronger. The timid little student that was before me, has changed into a desperate young woman. It makes my cock stir.

"Willow." I growl into the kiss. Her fingers jump to my shirt buttons, but I quickly hold her hands together.

"No." I finally manage to spit out.

She slowly shakes her head, never letting her lips leave mine, "Yes."

"No." I repeat, more strained this time, "We can't. I am your Professor."

A sigh of defeat escapes her lips as she drops her gaze to the floor. Slowly, she removes herself from me and my body cries out in desperation. I want her back on me, straddling me. I crave her touch and taste again.

"Oh." She whispers sadly. I can't help but use my thumb to tilt her head up so that she meets my eyes.

"I'm sorry, Willow." I tell her, "That shouldn't have happened. You cannot tell anybody about this."

I pull back from her like she's burnt me. I know that if I stay near her any longer, I will kiss her again and jeopardise my entire career and disguised reason for being near Emily.

"I understand." She nods her head slowly. A blush of humiliation coats those soft cheeks and she bites her lower lip. It is so swollen from our kiss. *Fuck!*

I clear my throat and put more distance between us.

"I will see you at our next lecture, okay?" I tell her uncertainly. She nods quickly.

"Yes, Sir." She says, still not meeting my eyes. My body groans

71

at the nickname. The naughtiness of the situation makes it that much hotter. But I can't. She is vulnerable, she doesn't need this type of complicated relationship in her life. Her main priority should be getting better. Passing her exams. *Not* sleeping with her professor.

The weight of the situation slowly seeps in. I flee the room before I can change my mind. My heart races as I storm out of the flat and down those creaky stairs. And even as I throw my car into drive and skid away from the building, I can still taste her on my lips. I still long for more. Like a lion who has tasted the blood of a gazelle, I crave more. But I cannot act on it. I will not act upon it.

And all I can do now is pray that she will keep our secret safe.

# CHAPTER NINE

## Willow's Pov:

Why did I open up to him? Why would I confess my conspiracy theory that my Doctor is out to get me? Why would I show the world my craziness? And why the fuck did he kiss me after learning my truth? Surely, he should be repulsed. Mortified. *Terrified*! This kind of confession would send others running for the hills.

"Hey, Kiddo." My brother walks into my room. The bags under his eyes are potent. Dark and red. Its only get worse.

"How are you feeling?" He raises an eyebrow up at me. I shuffle upwards in my bed.

"Jake, I didn't try to..." I begin but he quickly cuts me off.

"It doesn't matter what happened, as long as you're safe now." He interrupts before throwing my curtains open. The daylight shines through my dark room and hurts my eyes.

"I have to work an extra shift tonight. Do you think you'll be alright home alone? I know that you shouldn't really be alone at the moment, but I can't pass up the extra money. Then again, just say the words and I will stay home with you." He turns to face me. In the light, he looks much more exhausted.

"Maybe you should just rest, Jake." I push the covers back and pull my brother's hands into mine, "You look awful. You need to sleep."

"No," He shakes his head, "We need the money."

"I can get a job. I've offered before and I'll offer again. Jake, I can work at the campus or something?" I tug on his hands desperately. I can't keep letting him go to work and work himself into destruction. At some point I must help out.

"No." He doesn't even ponder on the idea, "Your job is to pass your degree and get us out of this shit town. Got it? It's my turn for the hard work, yours comes later."

I bob my head obediently. That has always been the plan, I just wished he would let me help him now. Miserably, I peer around at my disgusting room. More guilt eats at me. It's not like I would be able to hold a secure job with my mental health being this bad.

A chime rings around the room. I tear my gaze towards the Nokia brick on the bed.

"You got a phone?" Jake stiffens. Suddenly, a smile replaces the grim line on his face. He grabs it from the bed and checks it out.

"I could have gotten you a better phone than this." He frowns, "This thing looks ancient."

I pull it from his hands defensively. I knew that Jake would have spent his own money getting me a flashy phone to keep up with the young adult appearances. I did not want that. For the time being, I am satisfied with only Olivia's number in my phone.

*Perhaps Mr Anderson's number would work too...*

I force the thought out of my head.

"Why the change of heart?" He raises an eyebrow at me before busying himself with making my bed. I longingly watch at he gets rid of the comfy spot I was just in.

"A girl at school gave me her number, she wants to be friends." I tell him slowly. Shocked, he spins around to me with a huge grin on his face.

"Willow, that's great news!" He tells me proudly. I avert my eyes as a blush coats my cheeks. My phone chimes again so I check the message.

Olivia: *Party tonight at a house around the back of the University. Be there and wear something cute. X*

Olivia: *?*

I scowl down at the message. Why is she being friendly with me? What does she have to gain?

"What does it say?" Jake tries to look over at the message nosily. I pull it away from his face and hug it protectively against my chest.

"The girl I was telling you about. She invited me to a party tonight." I stutter in disbelief.

"That's great, Willow!" He beams, pulling me into an embrace, "You have to go. It's the perfect opportunity to make friends with people on campus. To have a normal life!"

I bite my lower lip nervously.

"I don't have anything to wear." I whisper with humiliation. Jake pulls back from me and quickly digs down my carboard boxes. Quietly, I take a seat on the bed and wait for him to find what he is searching for.

"Ah, here it is." He beams, pulling a dark, mesh top from the bottom of the box. My jaw drops.

"Jake, where did you get this?" I gawp, pulling the top into my fingers. Instantly, I press it to my nose; it doesn't smell of smoke.

"The firemen salvaged some of your clothes as your room was the last to burn." He tells me, "I had it dry cleaned. It has always been here. Why do you think I kept bugging you to open these boxes?"

A wide smile licks my lips. I could wear that top with jeans and my black boots, and it will look like I've made some effort. My smile falters.

"But what if the other students…" I start to speak my anxieties, but my brother hushes me.

"Don't." He tells me firmly, "Don't start with the what ifs. Just go tonight. You never know, you might like it. It might make you… *happier*."

He says that last word with such desperation. My heart skips a beat in my chest. My own brother doesn't believe that I am not suicidal. He believes the doctors and policemen. A scoff falls past my lips. *Could I blame him? Would who trust a crazy person over a frontline worker?*

*Mr Anderson.*

A blush jumps to my cheeks. I desperately try to push the thought away again. He mustn't plague my thoughts. Not only had he kissed me and made me feel things I haven't felt for years, but he also believed me. When he touched me, It was as if I was a normal woman again. Without delusions, without insanity. Just a woman who can lust for a man. I want to chase this feeling. I want more.

A party could be the best way to find more.

"So, you're going to go?" My brother presses. I purse my lips and nod my head slowly.

"Fantastic!" He declares, "Well you better text her back then and let her know you're going!"

I quickly do as he says, shooting Olivia a thumbs up emoji. The three little dots appear to tell me she is writing. Then her message comes through.

Olivia: *See you at 7pm.*

Hope fills my chest. I check my watch. I have four hours until the party starts. Until then, I have a mission to make myself look like a semi-normal young woman, ready to party.

\* \* \*

By the time I find the place, the party is in full swing. Olivia stumbles up to me after noticing me across the home-made bar. It reeks of spilt vodka in here, and the floors are sticky. The house is huge, bigger than anything I could have imagined.

"You came!" She grins as she trips over her footing. My hands shoot out to steady her and she quickly allows me to hold her still. She thrusts a red plastic cup in my hands and drinks from her own. Nervously, I peer down at the liquid.

"What is it?" I frown.

"R-Rum and coke." Olivia slurs her words before she drains the cup and slams it on the counter next to us. As usual, she is wearing her typical gothic attire with chains and skulls. Her hair has been curled and she wears very dark makeup. I can't help but admire how beautiful she is.

"No thank you." I tell her, handing the cup back. Since being put onto my antipsychotics, I haven't mixed it with alcohol, and I sure as hell wasn't going to start tonight! Who knows what could happen?

"Yes." Olivia presses, pushing it back into my hands. Nervously, I peer around. Every other young adult seems to be too drunk to notice us. Too drunk to notice if my delusions play up. I bite my lower lip nervously. Perhaps one drink wouldn't hurt. Perhaps one drink could help my nerves.

"Okay." I finally relent before taking a small sip. The awful, bitter taste fills my senses and makes me gag. It's nothing like I've had before. The liquid drips from my lips and I resist the urge to spit the taste out.

"Oh, I forgot to tell you, I pour drinks like there is no tomorrow." She gives me a half grin, pulling me into an embrace. Clearly intoxicated, Olivia stumbles around, pulling me back into the crowd.

"You need to meet somebody." She tells me with a mischievous smirk. I do not pull back from her embrace despite the uncomfortable alcoholic smell wafting from her breath. She is the only person I know here; I'm not going to leave her side for an instant.

"Willow, this is Dylan." Olivia announces, pulling me in front of a scruffy haired stranger. His piercing blue eyes on his doe like face catch me. They widen as Olivia pushes me closer towards him. I stumble away from her and him.

"Sorry." I squeak, holding my hands up defensively. The boy's lips twitch upwards in a schoolboy grin, and he flashes me his pearly teeth. He is very good looking with scruffy blonde hair, and piercing blue eyes like the colour of the sea. A red tinge kisses his cheeks, contrasting his snowy skin. He is a head taller than me with a lean, athletic build which my eyes greedily lap up. He is handsome. Not Mr Anderson handsome, but he is almost there...

"Nice to meet you, Willow." He pulls my hand from my side and places a kiss on the back of it. All the while, his eyes never leave mine. My cheeks brighten in humiliation, and I quickly pull my hand away. He isn't discouraged as he lifts his head up.

"Dylan is in our English class." Olivia notes. My lips curl into an 'O' shape and I nod my head politely. I do my best to look interested.

"The best in the class." He sends a mischievous wink and surprisingly it makes me a little weak in the knees. I gulp down more of the alcohol, but it doesn't seem to help with my nerves.

"Anyways, I'm going to get more drinks. Who wants one?" Olivia's eyelids flutter open and shut as she struggles to remain conscious. I resist the urge to ask if she *needs* another drink. Dylan shakes his head and I quickly tell her no. She disappears into the crowd of people, and I mentally curse her for leaving me alone with a stranger.

Awkwardly, I peer down at the clock on my phone. *How long until I can make a polite get away?*

"No way." Dylan exclaims, "I haven't seen a Nokia brick in years! Ha! Where did you get one?"

My cheeks flush as I hide my phone into my back pocket.

"Asda." I say lamely. He reaches for my phone without asking and inspects it. Curiously, I watch him as he lifts the lid. He types something into my phone before handing it back to me.

"Here is my number in case you ever want to hang out." He tells me nonchalantly. I watch as his cheeks flush red, but he expertly hides it with another award-winning smile. I find myself grinning back.

"Thanks." I tell him politely before tucking my phone back away into my pocket. I feel like I should say something else. Perhaps a flirty comment, or maybe I could brush my hand against his arm? Fuck- Willow. *Flirt.* Do something that a normal woman would do. And yet my lips remain pursed together.

I wait for him to cast his eyes away with boredom, like every man I've ever spoken to does. I wait for his polite excuse to slip away into the crowd to find a sexier, more talkative girl. Desperate, I open my lips to blurt out anything, but he beats me to it.

"So which book is your favourite?"

"Book?" I squeak in shock.

Suddenly, I lurch forward. Something slams into my back and my knees buckle in shock. However, Dylan quickly catches me and holds me close to his chest. Protectively, his arms wrap around my back, and he pushes the body which crushed me away. My mouth quickly dries. I can't tell if it's because of the alcohol or not, but he looks at me with a desire. It's hungry and polite at the same time.

From behind me, the girl who fell over her feet and into my shoulder offers a drunk slur of an apology before staggering towards the door. I watch, rubbing my sore shoulder slightly, trying not to let it get to me. But it's Dylan's expression that captivates me. He looks down on me as if I'm the most curious creature ever and his gaze flicks between my eyes and lips.

*It's nothing like how Mr Anderson looks at me.* That gaze is alluring, dangerous, possessive. It's perfect *almost.* Fuck, Willow. *Stop thinking about him*

Spluttering, I pull myself out of Dylan's arms. At first, he tries to resist but he eventually lets me slip away from his grasp. At the same time, Olivia returns with three drinks. She hands one out to each of us.

"I know you said you didn't want a drink, but it was three for two." She smirks.

"Olivia, it's an open bar." Dylan rolls his eyes at his friend. They exchange a laugh between them. The sound actually brings a smile to my own lips. I look at them both and peer around myself at the packed party. For the first time in six months, I feel light. Like the weight of the world isn't suffocating me.

Perhaps there is hope in my road to recovery?

# CHAPTER TEN

## Mr Anderson's Pov:

A sea of zombies stare back at me. Mouths are dry, and hanging open slightly, and there is a dazed look in at least half of the students. Attendance is also shit. I recognise this look. There must have been a party last night.

Slowly, my gaze drifts to my watch, and then back up to the sea of faces. There's one face in particular that doesn't stare back – *Willow's.*

*Where is she? Will I need to go to her house again?*

This thought makes me groan. I don't know if it's with excitement or fear at what could happen if we have a *next time.* The shrill cry of the second bell yanks me out of my thoughts. With a slight sigh, I turn to the projector and click onto the slide.

"Okay, can everyone turn to page sixty-four." I instruct to the classroom, "You should have done yesterday's work at home. Today is a new day so new questions."

"Sorry we're late!" I hear Olivia's voice echo through the lecture hall. The sound of footsteps pulls me from my thoughts, and I glare at Olivia who rushes in. Closely following behind, Willow and a male student take their seats in the front row. This male student clutches at Willow's hand. My eyes latch onto the contact, and I feel my heart sink in my chest. My thoughts race one hundred miles an hour. *Who is this fucker? And why is he touching what is mine?*

*No!*

I scold myself and force myself to take a deep breath. *Not mine. A student. Not mine to have.* But even as I think the words, the bile at the back of my throat forms as my eyes can't dislodge from their hands.

"Nice of you to join us." I tell them bitterly. Willow's round eyes meet mine. It's like someone has punched me in the stomach. She is so beautiful it hurts. A small blush kisses her cheeks, but she averts her gaze before I can get a good look. She slips her hand out of the boy's hand and thankfully, he doesn't make another effort to touch her. Watching them carefully, I force myself to unclench my jaw, my knuckles throbbing from the force I'm clutching onto the desk in front of me.

"The task is on the board." I tell them bitterly, "Everyone has ten minutes to answer the questions on their computers," I hesitate and look to the scrap piece of paper in front of Willow, "or on paper, before we go through it in class."

She is the only person in this class who isn't typing away at a computer. It makes her that much more special. The scraggily haired boy next to her says something and she gives him a polite smile but doesn't answer. Next to her, Olivia leans forward and continues the conversation with him. She makes a wild gesture of her head exploding, and I catch the words *"never drinking again"* as she hisses them to her friends.

*Hungover*, I realise quickly. Heart in my stomach, I glance over at Willow. *Is she hungover as well?*

To my horror, the asshole beside her has slung an arm around her shoulders and is pulling her into his side. My poor willow, just as anxious ever, doesn't protest, but I notice the way her eyes nervously dart around, the way she shuffles slightly to get away.

My skin crawls at how uncomfortable she looks.

"Hands to ourselves!" I hear myself boom. Eyes from every corner of the lecture hall stare at me but I don't care. A slight tremble floods through my bones. I've only known this woman for two weeks and yet I'm hooked. I long to protect her. To have her.

Mortified, the boy quickly pulls away. He readjusts himself in the seat and hangs his head low. Beside him, Willow scowls at me. Her lips pull into a grim line as she stares at me, silently challenging me. I quickly look away, a guilty feeling swamping my stomach. She is not mine. She will never be mine. I cannot have her, so others should be allowed to have her instead. And yet I can't unclench my fucking fists.

The trio continue their conversation. I try to look interested in the book in front of me, but I can't help but eavesdrop. The whole lecture theatre hums with quiet chatter but I can just about pick up Olivia's voice, "What time did you leave the party last night?"

"We left at, what time was it again?" The man looks at Willow. My blood boils. *We?* Since when was there a *'we'*? There definitely wasn't one yesterday when she threw herself at me!

"Eleven? It wasn't late." Willow answers nervously as she rubs the back of her neck.

"That early?" Olivia gawps, "When did I get home?"

*I can answer that one for her,* I think bitterly. Olivia stumbled into our two-bedroom flat at about three thirty in the fucking morning. I could hear her stumbling around, smashing things, before eventually, I heard her being sick. Soon after, I heard the door go and she disappeared back out to the party. Or she passed out in a bush somewhere. All I know is that I didn't see her this morning when I was getting ready for work.

"I'm not sure." Willow shrugs, "How's your head?"

"Shit." Olivia hisses, leaning forward and resting her head against the desk. She tilts it at the other two, "Wait, did you go home together?"

I clear my throat and rise to my feet. I can't bear to hear the answer. I don't want to hear the fucking answer. *Is Willow that kind of girl?* To kiss you passionately before disappearing to another man's arms? When I look at her, I think *no*. And yet as another man cosy's up into her, I'm not sure. A lump forms in my throat.

*Is Willow another Emily? Am I doomed to always fall in love with women who want to hurt me?*

"Question one, who wants to answer it?" I bark to the class. I can feel my temper rising but I can't seem to keep it in check. Furiously, I tear my gaze to the mousey haired boy.

"You. What is your name?" I scowl at him. I know I shouldn't act on my jealousy, but I *am* furious. How could Willow do this to me? I know that *I* said we shouldn't do it again but...

"Dylan." The boy responds nervously. His eyes dart up to the questions on the board. Slowly, he nibbles on his lower lip. A small smile flickers on my lips. *I can't get mad at him for going near Willow, but I can be mad at him for not doing the work!*

"Have you written anything down yet?" I cross my arms, "You've had ten minutes to start."

His cheeks turn pink, and he hangs his head low.

"Innocent." I hear Willow's voice call out. My head snaps towards her and I scowl. *What is she on about?*

"The answer is innocent. The characters Jones, Aaronson and Rutherford didn't actually do the crimes they were accused of." She explains with an inscrutable expression. I stumble over my words before taking a deep breath.

"I didn't realise I was talking to you, Miss Langly." I say tightly. She arches an eyebrow at me, challenging me. A look of disbelief crosses her face, and then it switches, making my stomach drop. Heart in my mouth, I watch quietly as she dips her hand down and takes Dylan's hand in hers. The muscle in my jaw throbs.

*What the fuck is she doing?*

"Answer the next question." I spit at her. Her eyes momentarily leave mine to check the board, before they shoot back to me, deadlier. Angrier.

"The answer is he sold his wife and children out. The skeleton looking man in room 101 sells his family out to stop the pain."

My ears turn red. "And the next one."

She doesn't hesitate, "Julia was a symbol of sex and rebellion. She seduced Winston and got him arrested."

I falter when Olivia clears her throat, snapping me out of my ridiculous rage. Tight-lipped, I watch Willow as she tilts her head back cockily. She challenges me silently, knowing there is not much I can do in front of everyone else.

"Good." I spit out, before snapping my attention away from her. Dozens of confused faces stare back at me, patiently waiting for me to continue. I want to march out, or to march toward her and see her squirm under my glare. She wouldn't be so brave if we were alone.

With a locked jaw, I manage to bark orders at the class, "I want answers to every question. You have half an hour to write them out. Anybody who doesn't know an answer will be leaving my class. There are no excuses."

A low groan fills the room, but nobody dares to say anything else. I storm toward my desk and slouch in the chair, counting down from ten to calm my racing heart. Willow has pulled her hand away from Dylan now that she has made her point, but it doesn't matter. His touch is still on her skin. It should be mine.

Her eyes meet mine, and they are full of hate. Then, she stands up and storms out of the room, and I don't give up the opportunity to watch the way her hips sway side to side. I cast a glance around the room, but nobody noticed her dramatic exit, too lost in planning their answer to the difficult questions. So, I take my opportunity to slip out of the room too.

As soon as the door shuts behind me, I hear her. She is pacing back and forth, widely storming around in circles, muttering things under her breath. With an amused smirk, I lean against the lockers and watch her work herself up. Then, she notices me.

"You bastard!" She hisses, storming toward me. She raises her fist and throws it into my chest, but I don't react, much to her frustration. A tight squeal leaves her lips as she raises her other hand to do the same thing. My fingers quickly grab the offensive thing and I squeeze her hand shut easily. My other arm snaps around her waist and I lock her against my body.

"Say that again." My voice is low, threatening. Shock dances in her eyes but she doesn't let her face show it. Instead, she throws her head back and maintains eye contact.

"I called you a bastard. You're a jealous bast-"

She doesn't finish her sentence before I slam my lips against hers. She gasps into the kiss but doesn't pull back, and instead matches my intensity. A moan slips from her lips, and it goes straight to my cock. I can't help but grab at her ass, giving it a firm squeeze. She pulls her fingers free from my grasp and sinks them into my arms. I groan, enjoying the pain. She thinks she is winning, but I'm the one with her against my lips.

"I hate you." She hisses against my lips. It makes me smile. I almost want to tell her *good.*

"You told me no. You said we can't do this. So, why did you do that in there?" Her cheeks are flushed with anger, and desire.

There is a slight croak to my voice, "Just because I can't have you, doesn't mean you are not mine."

"I am not yours." She hisses, though her blush betrays her. My fingers tighten around her ass, and I raise a cocky eyebrow.

"What do you call this then? This little position we are in?"

"Grooming." She bites back. I flinch and then release her.

"Don't take it out on Dylan because you are jealous." She glares angrily at me, "He is a good guy. Don't pick on him."

The question slips from my lips before I can stop it, "Have you kissed him? Fucked him?"

She visibly flinches and her jaw slackens in shock, then she reaches up and slaps me around the face. I welcome the burn and even lean into her hand to get better contact.

"You are a bastard, Mr Anderson." Her voice is low and threatening, "I wish I never met you. You're too hot and cold."

I enjoy the fight, "Feelings mutual."

"So, stop kissing me then." She protests, and a cocky smile stains her lips. She thinks she has won the war.

I shake my head, "No." and then slam my lips back against hers. She might tell me she hates me but the way her fingers are curled into my hair and pulling me closer, screams an entirely different story. I itch to take things further. My body screams out to take her. To fuck her in the school corridor, but I resist.

I give myself another couple of seconds to enjoy the way she tastes, and how her moans are hot against my lips. Then, I reluctantly pull my lips away from hers.

"Get back to class." I order against her lips before giving her a light slap on her ass. She squeals but I don't miss the lustful look that floods her face.

*Fuck.*

I fist my fingers at my sides, trying to regain control. She slips past me, throwing her shoulder into my arm in the process. I let her get that hit. I deserve it.

*Hot and cold,* she called me. And fuck is she right. If only she knew the fight going on in my head: Willow or revenge. Every day my priorities change. It's not fair on her, it's not fair on me. We can't, we can't, we can't. But it's almost like I *must.* I long for her. I need her. She's like my oxygen, and I suffocate without her. And yet I barely know her.

How can two kisses melt my brain? Have my cock harder than brick? Fuck.

Miss Willow Langly seems to have her pretty little fingers fisted around my heart, and there is not much I can do about it.

After a couple of deep breaths, I return to my desk. Nobody even bats an eyelid as I retake my seat at the front of the class. Out of the corner of my eye, Willow blushes frantically as she picks up her pencil. Dylan leans over to talk to her, but she shuts the conversation down just as quickly as it started. With an amused smile, I enjoy the way her hair is messed up and how her lips are a dark shade of red and swollen. My cock stirs at the sight, and I thank the desk for shielding me.

The time goes by too slowly for my liking. My class are fucking stupid. Nobody knows the answers to my questions. Nobody except Willow whose hand remains in the air.

"Yes, Willow." I sigh exhaustedly.

She beams, "The answer is fear. Fear is what keeps the dystopian society in check."

"Very good."

She sinks back into her chair with a proud smile on her face. My timid little student seems to be just as hot and cold as me. One minute, she's quiet and shy, the next, she is challenging me in front of the entire class. Her unpredictability makes my cock stir.

Searching for a distraction, I cast my eyes toward the blank faces staring back at me. They look guilty. Confused. I bet if I took their laptops, there would be nothing written down.

"This simply isn't good enough." I suddenly explode, surprising myself, "You have all the materials. This is supposed to be a clever class, and I'm looking at a bunch of morons! Tomorrow, there will be an exam. If you do not get more than 60% you will be resitting this class."

Then, as if on cue, the bell shrieks out, signalling the end of the lesson. As usual, my eyes flicker to Willow who tenses up at the sound. She is getting better and better at hiding her sudden fear each time it rings, but I can still see the cracks in her mask. The loud noise frightens her. I long to discover why.

Next to her, Olivia stands up and stuff her things into her bag. She is lost in conversation with someone I've never seen before.

"Olivia!" I call out, and she ignores me.

With a tense jaw, I try again, "Oliva, can I have a word?"

Slowly, she turns to face me, and a guilty look covers her face. Then, a sly smile slips onto her lips.

"Yes Sir."

Patiently, I wait for the class to disperse, and they all do eventually, except for Olivia and Willow.

"Are we still having a session today?" Willow's soft voice really contrasts her outburst twenty minutes ago. The way she switches back and forth only spurs my excitement on.

I dismiss her with a hand, "No."

"No?" She jolts with surprise, "But the exams are..."

"Still two and a half months away." I interrupt, "You clearly know all the answers as you proved in today's session."

Her eyes widen in shock and her jaw slackens. I enjoy pressing her buttons. She thought she won back there, but I always have a hidden move up my sleeves.

"You can go now." I say before giving her a tight smile. Her ears burn red, and she crinkles her nose, but she doesn't say anything. It disappoints me. I long for her to protest, like she did earlier. *Fuck.* I want her to throw another punch and kiss the insults off her lips. Is that fucked up of me? I want to push her until she breaks, and then punish her for it.

Instead, she twists on her feet and storms out the room for a second time this session.

"The tension is *so* thick." Olivia mocks before jumping onto the desk table, making herself at home. I glare at her.

"Glad to see you're enjoying the University life." I growl, "Where were you last night?"

Her lips pull into a teasing line, "It's not my fault you look ancient so had to play the professor, and I, the young- and good-looking- student."

"Olivia." I warn and she rolls her eyes, "Fine. Yes. I was at a party. Sue me."

My lips pull into a straight line as she opens her laptop and types frantically away. I wait patiently for her to find the research she promised she would have, but she seems to enjoy the silence. A small smile tugs at her lips as she waves her mouse around. I roll my eyes and find myself glaring at the seat where Willow and that boy was. My fingers itch to turn into fists.

"So, what's the deal with Dylan?" I hear myself ask the question before I can stop myself. Instantly, I mentally punch myself for being so stupid. Olivia gawps up at me and a mischievous twinkle flickers around her eyes.

"I knew it." She beams, "I knew there was something going on between you two! She froze up too when I mentioned you."

"You mentioned me?" I frown, "What did she say?"

My heart races one hundred miles a minute. I can trust Olivia with helping me find Emily, after all, who else will know my wife better than her actual best friend? But I do not need to bring her up to date with my situation with Willow. She will only push me away from her, and I physically cannot stay away from Willow. No matter how hard I try. *And just the thought of that scrawny little asshole's hands on her makes my blood boil...*

"Back to Earth, Liam." She sings mockingly before snapping her fingers in front of my face. Shakily, I take a couple of deep breaths to cool my rising temper. I change the subject.

"Whatever." I sigh, running a hand over my face, "So what do you have? What is Emily doing in this town?"

"I don't know." Olivia confesses, "She keeps going to that therapy building. Do you think she is seeing a doctor there?"

"I bloody hope so. That bitch needs more therapy than anyone else." I growl.

"But then it just doesn't add up." She sighs, pushing the laptop towards me. I pull it onto my lap and replay the CCTV footage. My eyebrows pull into a scowl, but I don't ask how she got the video. By some illegal means, no doubt. And I need no knowledge of that.

Holding my breath, I click play.

Emily saunters into the building and heads over to the receptionist desk. She says a couple of words before looking frustrated. Her arms cross over her chest defensively and she brings her face closer towards the receptionist, clearly threatening her.

I watch with wide eyes.

"What is she saying?" I frown, "What is she asking for?"

"Or *who* is she looking for?" Olivia pipes up miserably. The lump in my throat grows and I shake my head. *Is this another tortured soul that Emily will pick up, use, and drop?*

"What is she doing in this town? I don't understand. Why is she now going to the therapy block? And how the fuck is she managing to avoid us so easily?" I rant, waving my hands around. Olivia shrugs.

"You know your wife as much as I know my old best friend. Nothing she does or says is uncalculated. Emily has a plan, but I don't know what and I don't know why." She sighs, "All we need to do is corner her, get the closure you need, and perhaps save the next poor soul she seduces, robs and dumps."

My mouth feels dry, and my head is dizzy. I know I should let her go. She is my past. And yet, how can I throw away ten years of marriage without any answers? Had she ever been faithful to me? Had she ever been in love with me? Who did she find that was that much better than me that she had to start the divorce process six months ago?

"Do we know where she went when she left town yet?" I frown, resting my cheek on my hand. Olivia bites her lower lip and holds the silence.

"She went back to her mums for a couple of weeks. And then I spoke to some…" She clears her throat, "*friends*, and they said she came back and forth, looking for something."

I don't bother asking who her friends were. Again, either some illegal activities are going on or Olivia is spreading her legs for revenge. I don't blame her. Emily slept and robbed her husband too. And he paid with his life.

*Suicide.* The most gut-wrenching way to go. Olivia knows first hand the damage that my spiteful ex wife can cause. Our revenge will be severe.

"What is she looking for?" I frown, "There is something funny about all this. She left our home town so suddenly, and now she shows up in the neighbouring town. What happened before she left? Did she rob or cheat with the wrong person? Is she in danger?"

"I hope so." Olivia says bitterly, "One day, a wife will kill that conniving mistress."

My lips purse together. I push the laptop back towards Olivia. She closes the lid and pops it back into her bag.

"That's all the information I got so far." She sighs, "I will follow up with the doctor's office and see if I can find anything."

I nod my head once and then twice, more confidently.

"So, now are you going to tell me about Willow?" She raises a teasing eyebrow. I feel myself pale.

"What do you mean?"

"Oh, come on, you were staring at each other all lesson. You became all jealous over Dylan. And she was furious when you actively ignored her." Olivia waves her hands around as she explains, "Not to mention you two slipping out of the room. Yes, I saw that."

"Shut up, Liv." I groan.

"No. If anything, I think I will continue," She announces before throwing her hand to her heart, "How romantic! Wronged ex-husband stalks abusive wife and falls in love on the way!"

"With a student." I note miserably before recoiling, "I am *not* in love with her. Don't say that. Dylan can have her."

It's true. I don't love her, but I feel *something.* Even as I say Dylan's name, the words feel like mush in my mouth and I long to pull them from the air.

Olivia scrunches her face up.

"Not really." She tells me, "Sure they have a date planned for tomorrow. But I don't think she's interested in him. She told me her brother is making her live the *student life*. Parties, friends and *boyfriends*."

My lip twitches and my fingers feel funny. They curl up into fists.

"A date?"

Olivia's face lights up and she punches me in the chest playfully, "And you have the nerve to say nothing is going on between you two."

"I am her Professor, we can't." I repeat the professional rhetoric. Perhaps if I say the words enough, I will start to believe them. Maybe then I will follow the rules. But then again, I have never followed the rules.

Olivia gawps at me, wide eyes, and slack jaw.

"You do realise you're not her *actual* Professor, right?" She scoffs, "Sure, yes, you have been a professor of English elsewhere. But she technically isn't your real student. We will be gone soon. Make the most of it."

"She is as long as we remain in this town looking for Emily." I growl. As much as I hate it, it is true. No number of justifications could permit my relationship with Willow. If found out, it could jeopardise this entire plan.

"Besides, I'm like twenty years older than her." I murmur miserably more to myself than to Olivia. She doesn't seem to pick up on it as she rises to her feet and yanks her bag onto her back. Olivia, though in her mid-thirties, could easily pass off for a twenty something year old. A mature student is what she is going for. She is thin, and all bones. Nobody bats an eyelid when noticing her sitting amongst the row of students. I almost wish I looked younger so I could equally blend in. Perhaps then Willow could be a reality instead of a sneaky stolen kiss here and there...

"Whatever, Romeo. I should get going to my next class." She says with a roll of her eyes. I don't watch her as she exits my classroom. Shame eats me up.

"Oh, and Liam?" She calls out at the doorway. I peer up from the documents in front of me that I was pretending to read. A knowing smirk crosses her devilish features.

"Perhaps you should ask her out." She raises a cheeky eyebrow up at me, "We really aren't staying here for long. Fuck the consequences."

# CHAPTER ELEVEN

*15 years ago.*

## Willow's Pov:

Something awakes me from my sleep. A noise or something. But it is gone as soon as it appears. A cold breeze chills the room, so I pull the covers up higher to cover my chin. My eyes flutter closed but I am awake now. There is no use trying for sleep again. My mouth feels dry. I peer up at my empty water bottle and then sigh.

Irritated, I throw my legs over the side of my bed and grab my bottle. I slip the bunny rabbit slippers onto my feet and tip toe out of my room. The whole house is silent. With my slippers on the carpet, I am practically invisible. I don't want to wake anyone up on my quest for water. Mum will be very mad if she has to come help me; she has to wake up extra early for work and needs all the sleep she can get.

My small hand barely wraps around the banister as I creep down the spiralling staircase. Not even a peep as I finally get to the bottom. It's a long way down and my heavy breathing shows this. I cuddle my arms around my chest as the house feels colder down here.

The darkness swallows the house up but a slither of light shines through in the distance. I avoid the kitchen and hug my water bottle under my arm. The light attracts me like a moth to the flame. I startle as a thud echoes around in the distance. My heartbeat races in my chest and I feel fuzzy inside.

"It isn't real." I tell myself quietly, "It's just your imagination."

But another thud quickly follows. This time, my bottom lip begins to wobble. I think back to my doctors' words for comfort: *Is anyone else reacting to the event? Is there any evidence that this is real? Am I feeling threatened?*

This doesn't reassure me. There is nobody around me to check whether this is actually happening or just my mind. I believe I can hear things, but yet again, my mind has played these kinds of tricks on me before. Lastly, perhaps I am feeling threatened in the dark.

*I don't want to be down here anymore.*

Nervously, I take a couple of steps backward to hurry my search for water, but fear keeps my eyes locked on the living room. I swear something is in there.

Suddenly, something scurries across the room. This time I freeze. The water bottle slips from my fingers and makes a huge thud. A small shadowy figure stops and rears its head in the direction. Suddenly, it charges at me. I stumble backwards and fall to the floor. The figure leaps into my lap and suddenly it isn't as big as it was in the shadows.

"Mr Fluffy!" I beam cuddling the ginger cat. It purrs in my lap and snuggles up into me. A smile spreads across my lips as I stroke the warm thing.

"How did you get in?" I ask him before looking up. Suddenly, another figure sprints across the dining room. This one exits out of the open back door, where the light is coming in. Pale coloured hair shimmies in the light beam. I freeze.

Then, I can't stay quiet any longer. I take a huge breath in until the air stings my lungs, and scream. The sound is piercing and makes Mr Fluffy scurry away in fear. I pull my legs to my chest and cry out for my parents. Suddenly, something slams over my mouth. I lurch forward and kick as hard as I can, all the while shrieking in fear. Enormous hands wrap around my body and hold me still. It's much stronger than I am.

"Willow! Willow!" My Dad's voice calls out. He holds me still, and I melt into his protective touch. Slowly, he removes his hand from my face. I twist in his arms and throw myself into his embrace. The sobs wrack through me.

"There was something in here with me!" I cry. His shirt grows damp with my tears. Reassuringly, he rubs my back and keeps me close.

"It's all in your imagination, Willow." He soothes me, "Nothing is going to hurt you."

"No! No, there was something here!"

"Willow," He peels me off him to get a better look at my snotty little face, "You should be asleep in bed. What are you doing down here?"

I desperately look around for my water bottle, but it isn't here.

"I was thirsty." I return my attention back to him before wiping my nose on the back of my arm.

"Okay." He tells me quietly, standing to his feet. He holds his hand out to me and I quickly take it.

"What did you see? I mean, what do you think you saw in that room?" My dad queries as he leads me into the kitchen. My lips pull downwards miserably.

"I don't know. Something pale." I tell him, "Mr Fluffy was here too. The back door was open, Dad. Something got in!"

Suddenly, he spins me around. My dad drops to his knees in front of me and his grip on my shoulders is tight. It hurts and I yelp.

"No." He spits sternly, "No, Willow."

97

My eyes widen in shock, "Yes, daddy, Mr Fluffy was here. I was playing with him, and then he ran away!"

"Stop it! Mr Fluffy has been dead for months. He couldn't have been here." He scowls angrily, "You are seeing things. Perhaps we need to get you another appointment with the doctor."

I shake my head frantically.

"No, Dad. That's impossible. I *felt* him, I heard him!" I tell him quickly, "He crawled in my lap. And then I saw the creature run out of the door."

"What creature?" He becomes stiff.

"The pale one, I've already told you!" I cry out. He pulls me close and holds me still.

"Let's keep this between us, okay?" He whispers as he strokes my hair. I frown into the embrace and begin to shake my head. The fear and adrenaline make me feel sick.

"Willow, trust me. Nobody likes a crazy person. Keep it to yourself, my love." He tells me. My eyebrows pull together. *What if Dad is right? What if Mr Fluffy and the Pale monster were both figments of my imagination? What if I am growing crazier and crazier by the day?*

I stare over his shoulder and out of the window. In the moonlight, the wooden fence which separates my house from my neighbours stands out. On one of the broken slacks at the top, Mr Fluffy balances. His ginger coat shines in the moon light and those dark, beady eyes never leave me. It's as if he is silently challenging me with his existence.

# CHAPTER TWELVE

## Willow's Pov:

*Present day:*

"Where is the bar?" Jake scowls as he lurches the car to the left. Startled, my hand shoots out to steady myself as we tear around the corner ridiculously fast. The old car cries out as he throws the breaks on. I jolt forward but quickly correct myself.

"On the left here." I tell him but I don't point. My brother isn't the best driver in the world, and I fear if I remove my hands from the seat belt and counter in front of me, I will go flying across the road.

The car shrieks as my brother pulls up outside the large bar. Beautiful purple flowers blossom on hanging baskets, sprinkled with some pink roses. A sheet of paper reading 'STAFF WANTED' flaps in the wind, hanging from every visible window. On top of the large, triangle roof above the door, the large neon letters display: 'The Bar'.

"You really weren't kidding when you told me its name." My brother scoffs, "How original."

"Thank you for the lift." I smile at him sweetly before quickly undoing my seat belt.

"Have fun with Dylan and Olivia. I can come pick you up after my shift is done if you are staying late. This won't be until midnight though." He tells me through burrowed eyebrows. He hasn't stopped watching me since I told him I had plans to go out with some friends. Desperately, he scans me to check that I'm alright.

"But of course, if there is any trouble, and I mean *any* trouble at all..." He warns, holding his hand in the air.

"Jake," I moan, "It'll be fine. I took extra medicine. Plus, Olivia and Dylan are nice people."

He bites his lower lip nervously before sighing.

"Okay, Kiddo." He sighs, "Go have fun. Drink lots. Kiss loads of boys. Or girls- I don't know what you're into. But just let your hair down a little, yes?"

I groan at how embarrassing this conversation is. Since our parents passed away, it is a no brainer that Jake has stepped up to be the new guardian. This means awkward conversations and all. Even at my twenty-two years of age to his twenty-five.

"Promise." I tell him with a smile. He sends me a wink before throwing the car into drive. With a honk of his horn, he sends the car flying around the corner much too fast. I wince, waiting for the red tin of shit to fly into the bushes. By some miracle, he makes it back onto the main road without a scratch.

I pull on my leather jacket to bring me some sort of confidence before heading through the big, wooden doors. Inside, the smell of spilt alcohol fills my nose instantly. To the left of the room, a multi-coloured dance floor with a bunch of swaying bodies on it. I head toward the huge bar, figuring I could stand awkwardly by it until the others arrive.

"What can I get you?" Dylan's voice takes me by surprise. I jolt and turn to face him. Before I can react, he pulls me into an embrace. I let him hold me, but I do not hug him back. After a while, I manage to slide out of his grip.

"Just an orange juice." I smile politely.

"No alcohol?" He raises an eyebrow up at me. I scan the half-empty room and gulp. If I had a delusion here, it would be too obvious.

"No, thank you." I tell him, holding my hands up. Thankfully, he doesn't protest and instead turns to the barmaid before ordering our drinks. A song by Rihanna comes on and the bodies on the dancefloor go wild. They each jump against each other and hold imaginary microphones as they sing. I can't help but smile. It is only seven O'clock and they seem wasted.

"Here you go." Dylan says as he passes me my orange juice. I thank him before climbing up onto the bar stool.

"Do you know where Olivia is?" I ask him before sipping at my juice. A blush coats his cheeks, and he offers me a boyish grin.

"I told her an hour later than planned." He confesses. My eyebrows touch as I scowl, "Why would you do that?"

"I want to get to know you a little more. To give us some alone time." He explains with a small smile. My lip twitches and I can't help the disgusted look on my face. It isn't Dylan himself- he is a very good-looking boy. And perhaps in another life I would be very happy with him. But how can I try to date when I'm still broken? And when my mind is locked on someone else: *Mr Anderson*. Someone who doesn't want me. Who *can't* have me. Who kissed me and then pushed me away as if I was some whore.

Something in his eye flickers and his face falls, "Although now I realise that that was probably not okay…"

"No, it's fine." I lie.

Whatever is going on between Mr Anderson and me is too chaotic and unpredictable to understand. One minute he is picking on me, and the next he has me pressed up against a wall.

I should move on. Jake and Doctor Jane have been on my case about getting into a relationship. Due to the nature of my mental illness, I have never been able to hold a steady relationship down. Perhaps this is my new start. This is the new page in my book of healing. Dylan is offering me an opportunity too good to pass up.

"I'd like to get to know you too." I smile politely. His eyes widen and shoot between my face and my hand on his. Then, he quickly masks it with a cool exterior. He shuffles forward on his seat and leans forward, "So, tell me about yourself, Willow."

I shrug my shoulders, "What do you want to know?"

"Favourite colour?" He raises an eyebrow. I can't resist the laugh which tumbles from my lips. It is such an unexpected question. I almost welcome the light questions rather than your usual questions: *Where do you live? Are you close with your family?*

"Pink." I answer with a smile. He scoffs, "That is such a girly answer."

Playfully, I whack him on the arm, "Alright Mr stereotypes, what is *your* favourite colour?"

"That's not how twenty-one questions go." He scolds me, "It has to be a different question."

I bite my lower lip to stop the smile growing. My mind races for another light-hearted question.

"Favourite pet?" I finally say. He rests his head on his cheek and pretends to think really hard. It earns him another smile.

"That's easy. My dog- *Rex*." He confesses.

"Rex?" I scoff, "And you say I am stereotypical for liking pink. Everybody's dog is called Rex!"

A boyish grin plays on his lips as he shakes his head.

"It's okay when I do it, not you." He tells me teasingly. I can't help but think about how easy he is to get on with. It's so simple, almost *enjoyable*.

"Favourite book?" He raises an eyebrow. This question gets me thinking. I cock my head to the side as I race through all the books I've read recently.

"You know, I don't actually know." I frown.

"You have to pick one." He presses. I take another moment to think about my answer.

"Okay, fine." I finally relent, "It's going to be Brave New World."

He whistles and rocks back on his chair.

"Oh, so you're a dystopian type of girl." He grins, "I should have known."

"What's that supposed to mean?" I give him another playful hit. Only this time, he catches my hand. My legs slide between his as he pulls my chair closer. In my chest, my heart is going wild, my palms are sweaty from anticipation of what this handsome man is going to do next. For a moment, he just stares into my eyes, smiling gently.

And yet I *can't*.

I break the gaze first and awkwardly shuffle backwards. Something within me longs for me to want him. I want to desire him. He is perfect; funny, good-looking, not so serious. And yet he is no Mr Anderson.

"Ah, sorry..." Dylan starts but he is quickly cut off. Olivia bounces into view.

"Olivia!" He gasps, "You're early?"

Frantically, he checks his watch. She wears a twisted smile on her lips and gives him a pointed look.

"No, you two are early. It's a good thing I have you on *find friends*, Dylan, isn't it?" She tells him tightly before leaning between us, over to the bar maid. She barks her order before dragging a bar stool between us. I am grateful for the distance but at the same time miserable. On the one hand, it avoids any more awkward moves from Dylan. On the other hand, I wanted to trick myself into fancying him. Perhaps if I am close enough, talk to him enough, try enough that he will be... well, *enough*.

"What are we talking about?" She chirps merrily. I bring the straw to my lips and sip at my juice.

"Twenty-one questions." Dylan says quietly. It is clear that he has lost his confidence and spark. Olivia's face contorts.

"Why?" She scoffs before grabbing her own drink from the side behind her. She tips the bottom up and greedily gulps the alcohol down.

"It doesn't matter." Dylan says miserably. It pulls at my heart strings and makes me feel guilty. But not guilty enough to do anything about it.

"Anyways, what about tomorrow's exam, eh?" Olivia scowls into her empty cup.

"It sucks." Dylan rolls his eyes, "Why would he do that? None of us are ready for an assessment!"

"You're telling me." She agrees with him, folding her arms. Spurred on, Dylan continues his rant, "I mean, if you ask me, if the whole class is failing, that says more about the teacher than the students."

"In his defence." I chirp up before I can stop myself, "I knew the information. It is all in the booklet he sent out at the beginning of term."

Dylan jolts as I come to Mr Anderson's defence. I immediately kick myself. Students don't side with the teacher. We side with each other. I close my lips before I can say anything more damning. Beside me, Olivia's lips twitch up into a smile. It quickly falls. But I catch the movement.

"What do you think the exam will be on?" I change the subject, looking towards Olivia expectantly.

"Oh, my bet is on room 101. It will be about your worst fears." She sighs before clicking her fingers at the barmaid for another drink. The barmaid scrunches her face up at the rude gesture but doesn't protest. Instead, she rushes to complete the order.

I frown down at the orange drink between my fingers. Would

I be brave enough to open up to Mr Anderson about my worst fears? About my delusions taking hold of my reality? About being that crazy girl that everyone avoids? Probably not.

"What an odd question." Dylan sighs, "I wouldn't even know where to start. I'm afraid of everything."

He lightens the mood, and it works slightly. I smile at him. It perks him up a little.

"Why would he surprise us with the exam though? What got in his pants- or rather, what is *not* getting in his pants? Hah!" Olivia scoffs, her eyes never leaving my face. I choke on my juice at the abruptness. Dylan reaches over to pat my back as I sputter around like a fool. After what feels like an eternity, I regain my composure.

"No way, he is married after all. Married people never get laid." Dylan rolls his eyes.

My heart freezes in my chest. Startled, I tear my gaze around to him.

"Mr Anderson is married?" I can't help the question. I must know the answer. *Have I kissed a married man? Fuck!*

Beside me, Olivia's eyes are wide. She glares at Dylan.

"How do you know that?"

"Are you kidding me?" He scoffs, "Look at the man. He's good looking, has a good career and is in his late thirties. Of course, he is married."

"He might be divorced." Olivia perks up quickly, holding her finger in the air. I desperately try to get the air into my lungs. It is all too much. Perhaps that is why Mr Anderson didn't want to pursue anything further. It had nothing to do with his duty as a professor, and everything to do with the fact he is fucking married!

"Not a chance." Dylan shakes his head, "He worked at the University of Bristol. One of my mates transferred from there and instantly recognised him. She knew his wife too at the time. My mate recons she has seen the wife around here too. They must still be married."

My lips part and my heart feels heavy. I can't even hide my disappointment. I feel dirty. Used. Guilty.

"You know what." I say as I stumble to my feet, "I am not feeling too good. Perhaps I should go home."

I clutch my stomach and feign pains. Dylan jumps to his feet with wide eyes.

"Let me walk you home?" He lifts an eyebrow. I shake my head once and then twice.

"No, I am going to call my brother." I lie.

"Oh, okay." He says as his face falls, "Get home safe."

I nod at him and give him my best smile before glancing at Olivia. She looks pale and bites her lower lip nervously. It looks as if she wants to say something, but she doesn't open her mouth.

"See you tomorrow." I tell them both before exiting the bar. My heart races one hundred miles per hour and the sweat coats my skin. The shakes take hold of me and for some weird reason, the tears in my eyes threaten to spill.

Why am I so upset about him? He is my professor- nothing more, nothing less.

*It's because when he kissed you, you felt alive. In that moment, you didn't doubt fantasy from reality. It was a kiss of truth and passion.* The voice in the back of my head offers. It makes me tremble more. I hate this truth. I hate that Mr Anderson and his kiss has me under some sort of fucking spell.

# CHAPTER THIRTEEN

## Mr Anderson's Pov:

I can still smell the vanilla perfume which she used to wear all the time. Two pumps on her neck, one on each wrist and then one on each ankle. A true seductress move. She knew how to keep men hooked.

Those bright red lips which would curve upwards into a stunning grin when you gave her something that she wanted. Her long, dark lashes which would bat once. Twice. You'd go running. Scarlet cheeks and a sharp jaw line. You'd be on your knees.

One hand in your hair, the other pushing your chin upwards. She'd force you to make eye contact. A tear would slip down your face as you look up at the little devil. Moments before, she would have broken your heart. Told you a story about where she just was. *Who* she was with. My wife never kept her affairs secret. If anything, she enjoyed causing me pain. She enjoyed twisting the knife more and more in my heart.

Why didn't I leave? Why *couldn't* I leave? What fucking spell did she have on me?

The first time I found out about her disloyalty I cried for days at a time. It wasn't long after our wedding day; though, we didn't wait too long to say our vows. When I first laid eyes on her, I knew that she was the one. Something in your brain clicks when you meet the right person. I was intoxicated by her. She made sure to wear a satin, pale dress when she told me the traitorous news. It mimicked her wedding dress.

Her hair had been pinned back and for the first time in ages, her makeup was simple, elegant. Not once did she fall to her knees. Not once did she shed a tear. Not once did she apologise.

*"Liam."* She said as she shut the bedroom door behind her. I peered up from my marking. She looked so beautiful as she crossed the room.

"I've done something bad." She whispered. I ignorantly smiled up at her with not a care in the world. In that moment, nothing she could have said would have hurt me. She was the love of my life. My enduring happiness. With a wicked, small smile, she pushed me onto the bed and straddled me. Underneath her, I was defenceless. *How can you push her away when you wanted to pull her closer?*

"I cheated." She confessed. Not a single ounce of remorse danced in her devilish eyes. If anything, she scanned my face for a reaction. Of course, I didn't believe her. My wife, my lover, would never do anything as to hurt me.

"I cheated, Liam. I slept with another man." She pushed further. The smile on my lips faltered and my eyebrows burrowed together. The thoughts raced around my brain, desperately searching for whatever sick joke she was playing on me. I couldn't believe it. I wouldn't believe it.

"And I liked it." She licked her lips. This got a reaction from me.

"What?" My voice was small, desperate, broken. Her lip curved upwards in a wicked smile when she got the reaction she wanted.

"Who?" I croaked as the tears stained my cheeks.

"It doesn't matter." She told me.

But it did matter. Not long after, the first man she had an affair with took his own life. He was too infatuated with her, that he couldn't be away from her. His wife found him hanging in the bedroom with a one worded note: *Emily*. Soon after that, Olivia contacted me. We began a beautiful friendship of never-ending plans of revenge against my Wife. Against the so-called best friend who seduced her husband.

It never worked though. Whenever I grew strong enough to confront my wife, she drew me back into her charms. As if I was cursed, she had me falling to my knees with one word. Without her, I grew sick, weak, crazy. I needed Emily in my life to be whole.

And then she left me for good. Six months ago. Now I'm left to sitting in a miserably hot car on my Sunday morning, clutching a cold coffee, waiting for her to leave the doctor's office. Beside me, Olivia shuffles uncomfortably in the seat and sighs.

"It's going to be a long day." She huffs, checking her watch. I roll my eyes. Olivia has never been very patient with our stake outs. But they are crucial if we are to learn more about this wicked woman. This undetected criminal.

"How was your night the other night? I haven't seen you for ages." I make conversation. Anything to distract her from her moaning.

"Good." She says a little too quickly. I twist in the seat to face her.

"Just good?" I frown. She bites her lower lip nervously and she refuses to make eye contact with me. I cock my head to the side. Olivia has a nervous twitch of playing with her wedding ring whenever she lies. Right now, she twiddles that thing like there is no tomorrow.

"Olivia." I press.

"Okay," She quickly relents, "Willow thinks you are married."

"What!" I shriek, shooting forward in my chair. My cold coffee slips from my hands and explodes against my jeans before seeping down to the pedals. I don't even bat my eyelids at it.

"What the fuck do you mean?" I hiss, "Did you tell her?"

"No, Dylan did." She answers nervously. She throws her hands around dramatically, "I tried to lie and say that you might be divorced but I couldn't say much without it being obvious that I was defending you for some weird reason!"

I slam my hand into the steering wheel. So *that* is why she didn't show up to class on Friday.

"Why didn't you tell me sooner?" I growl, my temper rising. She shakes her head quickly.

"No," She hisses, "That isn't fair. This isn't my fault! He was either going to tell her in front of me or without me!"

"Why were they together?" I spit the question out. I think back to the way he touched her the other day in the lecture theatre. Then I remember Olivia telling me that they were going to go on a *date.* I didn't think Willow would have gone.

My blood boils.

"You can't control her, Liam." She frowns at me. A disgusted look crosses her face as she throws herself back in her seat. To an extent, she is right. I can't control Willow. I will not control Willow. And yet a part of me wants to scoop her up and never let another man look at her again. She is mine.

"Whatever." I huff, twisting back in my seat.

"Great and now we get to sit in silence for ages whilst you sulk over a woman you didn't even want a couple of days ago." Olivia can't resist but send a dig my way. A low growl escapes my lips, but I don't play into her game anymore. She will be looking for a reaction. A drama. It's a classic Olivia move.

"Or not." She frowns, falling forward. My eyes follow her gaze.

On the other side of the carpark, Emily walks out of the Doctor's building. She wears oversized sunglasses and a large hat, as if she is trying to hide her identity. Quickly, she hurries over to her car.

*The car she bought with the money she stole from me.* She unlocks it, leans in to grab something before turning around and hurrying back into the building. I waste no time charging out of my own car.

"Be careful, Liam!" Olivia hisses after me but I respond to her by slamming the door in her face. The cold autumn wind nips at my skin as I chase my ex-wife.

I quickly close the gap, ensuring I'm just out of sight. Slowly, I creep around the pharmacy corner, and watch as she marches up to the counter as if she owns the place. She slams her prescription letter down on the table and taps her foot impatiently. The scrawny looking pharmacist behind the counter grabs the slip of paper and scrambles around to get her pills.

I remain frozen as I watch her fold her arms and sigh. She rudely checks her watch and the tapping of her shoes grow louder and louder.

"Here you go, Miss." The pharmacist says as he returns, "Can you confirm your date of birth please, miss?

I don't let her answer as I barge in. I grab the arm which reaches for the pills. Startled, Emily swings around to face me. She instantly pales and her jaw slackens.

"What are you doing, Emily?" I hiss at her. She tears her eyes around to the customers who all watch us in shock.

"Get off me! I don't know you!" She cries out and tries to pull away. A menacing scoff leaves my lips, "Don't you? If I recall correctly, you married me!"

"Help! Help!" She calls out to the people around us. My eyebrows burrow together as the pharmacist jumps over the counter. I smack the pills out of her hand. They hit the floor and all the little pills explode out. They make lots of noise as they roll around. I drop to the ground and scoop up one in my hand, hiding it in my pocket, before she can see.

"Please leave, Sir. You are not welcome here!" The pharmacist demands. I turn to face the scrawny man who is now bright red. He trembles and tries to size me up but I'm much bigger and stronger. The anger races through me. Though I would never hit a woman, I'd make a good fucking exception for my wife. She isn't mortal. She is Satan incarnate- I'm sure of it.

A smug look rests on her face as the pharmacist lays a hand against my back to urge me out of the pharmacy.

"This isn't over." I growl before stumbling away from her. She plasters a fake frightened look to her face when everyone looks at her. But the minute they look back at me, her smugness returns. She sends me a wink followed by a kiss. My fingers itch to smack it off her face.

"Sir, now please!" The pharmacist tries again. My eye twitches and I take another step back. I raise my hands in the air.

"Fine, fine!" I hiss before storming out of the pharmacy. Nervous that they might call security, I race back to my car. I don't even bother to put my seatbelt on as I speed out of the carpark. My heartbeat pounds in my ears and the nausea consumes me.

"What? That was quick!" Olivia hisses as she steadies herself in the seat. I reach one hand into my pocket and pull out the pill. With a scowl, she takes it from my fingers.

"She was getting these pills. Any clue what they are?" I explain as I throw the car around the bend and out onto the main road. I check my mirrors to make sure we are not being followed.

"A red and yellow pill? No clue. It could be for anything." She shakes her head in despair.

"Well don't you have someone you could ask?" I blurt out in despair, "Anyone? Doesn't have to be legal, Olivia!"

"Now you want their help." She snarls, clearly not over our previous argument. My fist drives into the car radio system in frustration. The adrenaline pulses waves and waves through me. I can't believe I let Emily play me like that in there. No doubt she is playing the victim card and getting as much attention as she possible can out of it. She might even set the police on me and get a restraining order. Of course, it will be behind the pretence of another identity. That sneaky little bitch.

"Please, Olivia." I beg, calming down slightly, "Is it possible to figure out what these are for?"

A long silence hums between us. Eventually, she sighs and pulls out her phone. She takes a photo of the pill and sends a message to a couple of different contacts.

"I will send it in for testing too. But it could take a couple days, even weeks perhaps." She tells me.

"Weeks?" I breathe out in despair, "We don't have weeks. She knows I am here now!"

"You should have waited!" Olivia explodes, "But no! You let that hot head of yours get the better of you! And now look at us, for fuckssake!"

"What did you want me to do?" I shriek, matching her energy, "She took everything from me, Olivia! I only just stopped getting the shakes and night sweats! She has drained me of everything!"

"At least you're still alive." Olivia drops her voice a couple levels. My lips purse shut. As much as I hate to admit it, she is right. I might have been completely destroyed, but I at least have a foundation level to grow on. Her husband does not have that luxury.

Shakily, I take a deep breath in and out. My hand rests on her knee and I give it a reassuring squeeze.

"I'm sorry, Liv. I shouldn't take this out on you. I shouldn't have acted so irrationally there. That is my fault." I apologise to her. Her lip twitches upwards and she bows her head.

"Thank you, Liam." She whispers, "I know this isn't easy for you."

A lump forms in my throat. That is an understatement.

"It's just more of a reason why we need to bring the bitch down." She finally says after a long silence. I hold my fist out and she pumps it with her own fist. And just like that, our tiff is forgotten, and our plans for revenge grow more intense.

# CHAPTER FOURTEEN

## Willow's Pov:

"How are you feeling this week?" Doctor Jane smiles politely as soon as I sit down in my usual chair. I don't answer her. Instead, I look helplessly towards the bars which have been installed around the windows. A lump forms in my throat.

"I wasn't going to jump." I tell her numbly. For a couple of moments, she is silent.

"It is a precaution." She answers cryptically. My fingers twitch with anger towards Doctor Jane. How dare she assume I was going to jump? If she had just listened to me, she would have known I just needed air. *Is it criminal to open a window?*

"Anyways, your exams are approaching, how does that make you feel?" She tries to talk about education, but I shut it down again. I will not discuss the catch-up sessions nor the lectures. I am not here to talk about school. I need to get this healing shit over and done with.

"I made new friends." I tell her half confidently. Her face lights up and a sense of pride floods through her expressions.

"Olivia and Dylan." I explain, "We hang out a lot."

"That's great, Willow." She beams, "Are they course mates?"

"Yes."

"And how does it make you feel, knowing that you've successfully made friends at University?" She pushes the conversation into the direction of my feelings. I gulp and peer down at my fingers.

"I think Dylan likes me." I whisper, "*Like* likes me."

"And do you like him back?" Doctor Jane raises a suggestive eyebrow. I purse my lips and look up at her weakly. From her facial expressions alone, I can tell she wants to hear the answer *yes*. Her, my brother and my head- all of them are gunning for team Dylan. And yet my heart is still set on Mr Anderson for some mysterious reason.

"Sure, he's nice enough." I sigh, rocking back in my seat. When I peer up again, my mother has joined us in the therapy room. As usual, she stands behind my therapist. Her long flowing hair cascades down her back and hugs her pale coloured dress. Her face is blurred out, like a swirling hole. But I know it is her. I can feel it is her. Mum's fists are clenched at her sides, and she pants. I frown at her strange behaviour.

"And your delusions..." Doctor Jane starts, peering down at her folder. My mum leans over to look at the notes too. Slowly, she shakes her head.

"How are they?" Doctor Jane peers up at me expectantly. Nervously, my eyes dart between her and my mother.

"Good." I lie.

"Are they better now that you are back on the medicine?" She raises an eyebrow.

"Sure." I lie again. Anxiously, I chew on the bottom of my lip. My mother straightens her back and despite her having no obvious eyes, I feel them attached to me. If she had facial features, I'm sure she'd be scowling at me. I can feel the adrenaline oozing out.

Suddenly, she twists her body in an unnatural way. Her bones seem to break and crack and a black tar pools around her bare feet. Mortified, I watch with wide eyes.

"Perhaps you should take another one." Doctor Jane tells me, noticing my sudden distress. She reaches into her bag and pulls out the pills. As she leans over the desk to pass it to me, my Mum charges. Suddenly, I'm hurling backwards.

When my eyes re-open, I am no longer in the therapy seat. Instead, I'm sat cross legged on my bed at home. My heartbeat accelerates as I tear my gaze around the room. I am alone. *But how did I get here?*

"Time." I pant to myself, "It is hard to understand."

My body feels heavy, and tired, and there is a textbook on my lap. Hesitantly, I push it to the side and swing my legs over the side of my bed. My hand covers my chest as if that will control my rapid heartbeat. As I stand from my bed, my phone rings. The sharp bells send another wave of adrenaline through me. Shakily, I press the phone to my ear.

"Willow?" Mr Anderson's voice echoes through the phone. I freeze on the spot and remain quiet. The sound of his breathing sends shivers through me. How did he get my number? Why is he calling me? Not only is he my teacher, but he is also married!

"Willow, I know you are there." He tries again. His voice cracks and a slither of desperation oozes through.

"Please." He begs, "Please answer me."

"How did you get this number?" I croak as I slump onto the floor. The lump in my throat forms. *Why is he tormenting me?*

"It doesn't matter, all that matters is that I want to see you. *Need* to see you." He whispers. The sound makes my heart skip a beat.

"You are married!" I half shriek.

"No, well yes, but it isn't what you think!" He quickly retorts, "Just… Just let me in, okay? I'm outside. I will explain it all."

I scramble to my feet and stick my head out the window. True to his word, Mr Anderson stands on the patchy grass, staring up at me. His beautiful face contorts into a painful expression.

"Am I allowed in?" He asks delicately. I am breathless as I respond, "Yes."

Hope flickers across his face. Before I know it, he is scouring the wall and drainpipes like there is no tomorrow. I watch in fear as he decides to climb up to my bedroom window. A part of me is thankful that he doesn't use the main door; Jake is asleep, and his bedroom is right next to the entrance way. He would definitely wake up, and I do not have the energy to tell my brother about my handsome teacher's affair.

"Open the window more." Mr Anderson calls out to me. It brings me back into reality. I throw myself forward and unlatch the window. It swings wide open. One of his large muscular arms shoot through, then another. His face is red, and he pants as he finally swings a leg over. With a thump, he falls onto my bed. I am speechless.

"Thanks." He sighs breathlessly. For a moment, he just lays there, staring up at my ceiling. He slowly catches his breath.

"You have a wife." I hiss, marching towards him, "You have a wife and you kissed me!"

Mr Anderson shoots up. I raise my fist and get ready to hit him around the face in despair. However, he is much quicker. He grabs my arms and yanks me closer. He wraps me into an embrace. At first, I struggle away but his usual smell of cigarettes and oak fill my nose and calm me down, despite my best efforts to remain angry. Weakly, my head rests against his chest. I feel the heat shoot to my cheeks and the tears sting my eyes.

"You're married." I whimper numbly.

"No, I am in the process of a divorce." He finally confesses. Slowly, he pulls us into a sitting position on the bed. He never lets me leave his embrace.

"My wife left me six months ago, though I'm sure she mentally clocked out before that." He whispers. A silence prevails between us. Slowly, I wiggle my way out of his hold.

"She left you?" I frown, "Why?"

"I don't know." He whispers before pursing his lips. A lost look flickers across his face. For the first time, he looks weak, out of control. His beard is stubbly, and eyes are heavy. It looks as if he hasn't been sleeping.

"But trust me, she is completely out of the picture." He finally sighs and makes eye contact again. I can't help the scoff, "That doesn't matter though because you don't want me. This is wrong, what is happening between us."

He looks as if he deflates with my words.

"No," He whispers, "How can it be wrong when it feels so right?"

"What?" I squeak.

"Willow, I cannot get you out of my head. I am obsessed with you. You are my waking thought and the last thing I think about before I go to bed. And even then, you're in my dreams." His face contorts as he tries to explain his feelings, "I can't help the attraction I have for you. And then I saw you with Dylan and..."

His fingers clench into fists.

"It solidified my feelings for you." He tells me tightly, "I don't want to be without you. University be damned."

"Mr Anderson." I hear myself whisper. He takes my hands gently in his own before shaking his head, "It's Liam."

I try his name in my head multiple times before a small smile teases my lips. It suits him so well. His eyes flicker down to my lips and suddenly it feels as If I am no longer breathing. I don't know whether I can trust what he is saying. What proof do I have that he is not married, and not just saying this to justify an affair? But as he slowly leans forward and my body responds to him, I no longer care.

Finally, our lips touch. It is nothing like our first kiss; this one is gentle, full of pain almost. Like the first kiss after a breakup. His hand slowly cups my face as he deepens the kiss. I moan in approval.

My arms snake around his neck as I pull myself closer to him. His hands jump to my legs, and he quickly wraps them around him. I gasp.

"Willow." He groans into my lips. The sound is so sensual, so endearing. Slowly, he lays me down on the bed. My eyes flutter close as he gently kisses down my neck, over my collar bone. His fingers fist the baggy t-shirt I'm wearing, and I mentally curse the barrier. Then, his hand slides up it. His soft kiss returns to my lips as those gentle fingers trail up towards my breasts.

"No bra." He breathes out. A smile coats my lips, but my lips quickly curve into an 'O' shape when his fingers connect with my nipple. Instantly, my body responds to him. My back arches into his touch and a long moan slips from my lips.

"Fuck." He growls into my ear. It only spurs me on more.

"Please, Liam." I beg, but I don't know what I'm begging for. *More!* My body screams.

That's it." He groans, "Say it, say my name again."

"Liam!" I respond quickly. How can I resist obeying him when he brings me such pleasure? Teasingly, one of his hands trail down my stomach. It stops at the waistline of my pyjama bottoms. Slowly, he runs a finger underneath the elastic band. His dark eyes scan my face for any indication to stop.

"Please." I whimper before throwing my hands to my trousers to try and remove them. Suddenly, he grabs both my wrists with one of his hands. He places them above my head. I moan out in surprise and desperation.

"Do not move your hands, understand?" He tells me sternly. His lips curl into a devilish smile. I think I might combust from that look alone. Unable to put my thoughts into words, I nod my head frantically.

"Good girl." He whispers before placing a kiss to my stomach. The touch makes all my hairs stand up. I squirm under him, but his strong hands keep me still. Slowly, he rearranges my shirt, over my head and wrap them around my wrists so I have no choice but to keep them locked together. I blush as my breasts bounce onto display. A hungry look flickers across his face as he licks his lips.

"God, Willow." He groans in approval. Suddenly, his tongue darts out and attacks one of my nipples. My back arches in pleasure and my eyes flutter shut. I can't even describe how good it feels as he begins to twiddle with the other one. Then he swaps, making sure they both get equal attention.

"Fuck, Liam." I whimper. Frustration takes hold of me at how close I am already just from my nipples being played with. I never want this moment to end.

Then he pulls back and removes my trousers. I lift my hips in the air to help him remove my trousers.

"No knickers?" He raises a suggestive eyebrow before placing a kiss on the top of my mound, "It's almost as if you were expecting me."

That comment sends another wave of heat between my legs. He shuffles down in the bed and parts my legs. Desperately, I let him take control of me. He blows on my clit and the cool air makes my back arch. I can't help but watch how sexy he looks between my legs.

"You're perfect." He whispers before placing a small kiss on my clit. I fall back onto the bed. Slowly, he runs his tongue through me. A long, guttural moan seeps from his lips.

"You taste so fucking good." He growls before throwing himself back into it. Suddenly, his slow sensual movements become faster, harder. Like a crazed animal, he feasts on me. My legs flail around in pleasure, and I fist the pillow above my head.

"Yes, yes, yes!" I hear myself chant in pleasure. It isn't long before

I'm almost falling off the edge.

"Liam, I'm going to…" I begin. Suddenly, he thrusts two fingers into me. This pounding alongside his fantastic tongue makes my eyes roll back in my head.

"That's it." He groans into my clit, "Cum for me, Willow."

Those devilish words are all I need. Before I know it, I'm falling over the edge. The trembles take a hold of my body, and a long moan escapes my lips. I convulse under his touch, and he doesn't seem to stop. He growls and the vibrations hit my clit. Quickly, I fall over the edge again. The pleasure is too much, I finally move my hands and push at his head to stop him. The sensitivity is too much!

"That's my girl." He groans, slowly pulling away. With hungry eyes, he stares down at me. I have never seen someone with that much desire before. He towers over me and soaks up me after shakes.

"Kiss me." He demands, "Kiss your cum off of my face."

I throw myself into the kiss, desperately. My hands snakes around his neck and I pull him close. He scoops me up into his lap and holds me firmly. Slowly, he pulls back.

"That was definitely worth the expulsion." He grins at me. I nod my head frantically. I couldn't have put it better myself.

# CHAPTER FIFTEEN

## Mr Anderson's Pov:

**M**y red pen scribbles a huge F on the written essay in front of me. I huff as I throw it to the side and pick up the next essay to be marked. The large pile of shit results rests to my left, and the unmarked essays are to my right. So far, nobody has done well. What is it with these students? It's like they don't care for their results!

I take another puff of my cigar and scowl down at the next essay. The handwriting is small and beautiful. I instantly recognise it. *Willow.*

Quickly, I check which essay question she selected from the choice of five.

"In 1984, the ruling party utilise a torture method called Room 101. If you were in room 101, what fear would they use against you? Describe it. 30 marks." I read the question out loud. Instantly, I'm intrigued. Is my mysterious little Willow going to confess her fears to me? Does she trust me with this secret?

I flip the front page over to reveal her work.

*In 1984, the ruling party utilise a torture method called Room 101. If you were in room 101, what fear would they use against you?*

## Describe it. 30 marks

*By Willow Langly*

*The question is challenging for one main reason: the torture methods in room 101 pull out your worst fears. That much is clear, but what isn't included in the title, is that room 101 involves your fear to the highest possible extent. For the party to evoke the most amount of suffering to the victim, their fears must be multiplied greatly. This leads to an enormous problem for me... My worst fears have already come true.*

*Now, I know what you are thinking: It isn't possible! Things could always be worse! But could they? I don't believe they can. That is of course unless I drop dead this very instant.*

*And isn't it great that within the book, Room 101 is located within the Ministry of Love. Ignoring the obvious analysis of satirical irony with Orwell mocking the state through using juxtapositions in his building titles, there is another interpretation. A better interpretation.*

*Love itself is a universal Room 101. Think about it. Which other emotion can deliver on every little wish, desire and happiness, making you feel above the world, only to then slaughter your fantasies. As lovers, you go from strangers to something more, to strangers again. How do you recover from this? Can you recover from this? Or will a part of your soul forever be indebted to the person you love? After a while, you hand out different parts of your soul to different people. It's all fun and games until you have nothing left to give. Then you are a shell of a person. Nothing more yet much less.*

*In school, you are not taught how to grieve this kind of loss. Or any loss for that matter. They say, 'chin up, buttercup' and push you back into reality. You are not allowed to mourn in your own way. God no! This is too awful for everybody. So, they put a knife at your back and tell you to walk the plank. Walk the plank to your mental death. Because it makes them look good. They are the hero! They made you return to reality! They have done a good job! And you? Well, you've lost another part of your soul.*

*And isn't it great that love can sell you out?*

*I mean, Orwell talks of it himself within the book. One man sentenced to Room 101 declares "I have a wife and three children" and yet the ministry could "take the whole lot of them and cut their throats in front of my eyes, and I'll stand by and watch it.". Isn't that lovely? Have you ever felt something like this, Professor? Like someone you love has sold you out. Because I have.*

*My throat has been cut, Professor. Sliced over and over again so it is now hard to breathe. Not physically cut. Symbolically. I have no voice. I have no voice, Professor. Do you understand this? You must understand this for me. It is vital in explaining why Room 101 is happening every day.*

*The people I love have sold me out and cut my throat, cut my voice. 'It's all in your head' they will tell me when I report something unusual happening. 'You're just delusional' is another great one. And sometimes even the harsh 'Don't be crazy! That didn't happen!'. Do you know what kind of things happen to a child who is told they must doubt every little thing they think they've seen and heard? It's no childhood- I can tell you that much.*

*Room 101 is introduced towards the end of the novel, but you know this already. My interest is in the idea that I am living in Room 101 every day of my life. Yet I can't tell whether this is the beginning of my life- will I get better? Or is this the finale? Perhaps I peaked as a child. Until the age of around ten, I had been a fairly normal child. No delusions, no psychotics. With both parents.*

*I don't know what changed and perhaps I never will. It is beside the point.*

*I've touched on Love; I've touched on fantasy. Now, let's look at reality.*

*What is real? It's a philosophical question. I shall be looking for the answer for every day for the rest of my life. A great example: Is this cat real or just part of my imagination? I can hear it purr. I can feel it's warm skin. It responds to my soft whispers. We could be there for hours, cuddled up, just enjoying each other's company. And then your dad walks into the kitchen and asks why you're laying in a heap on the floor. You tell him 'I'm playing with the cat!' and he responds, 'we don't have a cat?'. This doesn't deter you, of course. You know you don't have a cat. But the neighbours do! So, you tell him just that. He repeats his main objection 'They don't have a cat... anymore...'.*

*Look down at your lap. The cat is still there, purring, licking itself clean. With big beady eyes, it watches you. I know cats can't smile, but that one did. 'Can't you see it?' I gawped. He shakes his head once, then twice. Fine, that solves that mystery; the cat is part of your imagination.*

*So, tell me why later that day I watched my father enter the kitchen to start cooking dinner. The back door was open, and the cat returned. He bent over and gave it a scratch behind the ear. Lovingly, the cat purred. I can't tell you my shock when I watched that happen. But then again, can I really be sure that that wasn't in my imagination too?*

*Nobody understands the torture of constantly having to survey your surroundings. 'Is anyone else reacting to the event? Is there any evidence that this is real? Am I feeling threatened?'. These three questions get harder and harder the worse your mental illness gets.*

*I've said too much. Revealed too much. No. Perhaps I haven't.*

*Is this essay even real? Perhaps this is a part of your imagination.*

*In conclusion, Mr Anderson, this is what Room 101 is like for me. It is life itself.*

I rock back in my seat, mortified. My cigar ran out ages ago, perhaps after the third read of her essay. My chest rises and falls. Willow always had a way with words, but this was something next level. Usually, I would penalise a colloquial essay, but for her content, it suited it perfectly. It flowed so easily.

My red pen presses against the page. It creates a dark splodge of ink pouring out as I pause. What grade could you give someone who has poured their heart out to you in a poetic way whilst also explaining your own feelings and fears?

My pen delicately creates an 'A'.

I fall back in my chair and sigh. That essay took a huge mental toll on me. Willow might be more dangerous for me than first imagined.

As if on cue, she appears at the door to my lecture room. Her nervous posture and low gaze tell me she remembers the other night all too well. With a gulp, I sit up right.

"Come in." I try to sound formal, but my voice is low as flashes of memories of our time together flicker across my mind. As she enters the room, my gaze falls to her breasts, unable to resist a peak again. When she catches me staring, I clear my throat, shifting uncomfortably in my chair with a blush burning my cheeks.

However, she doesn't comment on my wondering eyes. Instead, she comes to a stop in front of my desk, wringing her hands anxiously in front of her.

"I was wondering if you have finished marking my essay, please? I'd like to give it to Doctor Jane. I think it will help her understand me a bit more." She whispers. A nervousness flickers across her face as she looks between the document in my fingers and my expression. I force myself to release the document from my tight grip.

"Of course." I say as I hand her the document. Anxiously, she opens the front page and checks her a grade. A look of pure excitement crosses her face.

"An A!" She squeals happily. The sound fills my heart up with joy and I can't help but smile.

"Of course." I nod quicky, "You deserve it. That was a beautifully written piece of work."

She hugs it to her chest as if it means the world to her. But then again, the good mark is almost a reassurance of her thoughts and feelings. In this split moment, I have offered her, her voice back.

"Thank you." She beams, "This is great!"

"It is indeed. It is very promising, especially with your exams coming up in a couple of weeks." I tell her with a small smile. At the mention of the exams, her smile falters slightly. I stand from my chair and walk around the desk towards her.

"Tell me," I whisper, a frown crossing my face, "Do you actually struggle to tell what is real and what is not?"

A long silence floats between us. Anxiously, she bobs her head. I can't help myself. I reach up and stroke her cheek.

"Am I real to you?" I mutter, getting lost in her dark eyes. She nods quickly.

"Of course, you are." She breathes out, taking another step towards me. Her arms slither around my neck as she pulls me close. Her smell is intoxicating and makes me feel dizzy. Slowly, I lean towards her until our lips are inches apart.

"Remind me." She whimpers, "Remind me how real you are."

I can't help the crazed emotion which floods through me. This woman could be the death of me. I slam our lips together in a heated kiss. My hands jump down to her legs, and I wrap them around my waist, before turning and resting her on the desk. She frantically undoes her buttoned top to free her breasts. This time, she is wearing a gorgeous, lacy bra. The baby pink contrasts her pale skin and makes my cock swell at the sight of it.

"Willow." I moan before kissing her again. Her fingers jump to my belt, and she quickly yanks it off and chucks it to the ground. Her desperation matches mine. Then she pushes me back slightly. I stumble backwards and watch the lustful look fluttering around her face.

Suddenly, she drops to her knees. My eyes widen in shock and desire.

"Willow, you don't have to…" I trail off. She shakes her head and fumbles with the buttons on my jeans.

"I want to." She whispers, "It's your turn to be pleasured."

I don't protest anymore. Instead, I lean up against my desk, my fingers clutching the wood. She pulls my trousers and pants down and my cock finally springs free.

"You're huge!" She gawps, staring up at me in disbelief. My expression is strained. How could I focus on words when those pretty lips were so close to my cock? I can feel her breath on it.

Slowly, she takes me in her fingers and gently starts pumping.

"God, Willow!" I growl as she speeds up. Then, she brings her lips to the tip of my cock and kisses it. A moan falls from her lips and the vibrations increase my desire. Her tongue darts out of her lips and she licks all the way up my shaft. At the same time, she thrusts my cock with her fingers. I gawp down at her in surprise. How does she know how to do this so well?

Her red lips wrap around my cock, and she starts sucking. The saliva mixed with precum gives her a slippery surface to bob her head faster and faster. My knuckles turn white as the grip on the desk becomes too much.

"Willow." I growl, "I'm close."

She moans in approval and speeds up. I feel the back of her throat constrict against my cock as she thrusts it all the way back. All the while, her eyes are staring up at me lovingly. She sends me a teasing wink. I can no longer hold back.

"Fuck." I grunt as I cum into her mouth. She licks it all up diligently, not wasting a drop. A slight tremble takes hold of me as I slowly come down from the high. She gives me one last kiss before standing to her lips. My heart races faster and faster, and I feel my cock swell back up again when she smiles innocently.

"Where did you learn that?" I whisper against her lips. A huge blush taints her cheeks as she shrugs.

"Nowhere." She squeaks nervously, "I've never done that before. I've just read about it I guess."

My heart drops. Gently, I pull her up against my chest. She rests her chin against me and peers up lovingly.

"Willow," I whisper, "Are you a virgin?"

Another blush stains those gorgeous, round cheeks. She nibbles on her bottom lip nervously before nodding her head. My stomach flips.

"Fuck." I groan in approval.

"Nobody wants to fuck a crazy girl." She mutters. For a moment, a flicker of hurt echoes across her face. I place a light kiss to her lips, but my smirk makes it difficult.

"I do." I whisper, "I want to fuck the crazy girl."

# CHAPTER SIXTEEN

## Willow's Pov:

T he smile is still glued to my lips as I unlock the front door. It creaks and slams open as the wind takes a hold of it. I stumble into my flat and lock the door behind me.
"Jake?" I call out, excitedly. My essay is crumpled from where I haven't put it down

"Jake?" I try again, bouncing into the kitchen. On the sofa, head in his hands, my brother sits. Miserably, he peers up at me. His eyes are red and puffy.

"What's wrong?" I whisper, advancing towards him. I throw my bag to the side and sit next to him.

"I lost my job." He sighs, "I knew they were cutting people, but I thought I was safe because of that raise…"

"Oh." I say weakly. He runs a hand through his matted hair and sighs again. Reassuringly, I throw an arm around him.

"Don't worry about it, Jake." I whisper, "We have some savings, and you can find another job in the meantime."

"No." He shakes his head and clears his throat, "We do not have enough to get us through the month. And barely anywhere is hiring."

I chew my lower lip nervously and watch as my brother begins pacing back and forth. He trembles and mutters to himself, desperately sorting out a plan.

"I mean they gave me a little severance fee but again, it isn't enough to cover rent." He huffs.

"Jake, that bar I was at the other day is hiring?" I tell him, thinking back to the dozens of littered pieces of papers.

"I'm not a student." He scowls, "They won't hire me."

"Well then, I'll get a job." I tell him sternly. His lips pull into a straight line, and he stops pacing. Soothingly, he rubs at his stubbly beard with the palm of his hand. For a moment, he considers my offer. Then he shakes his head, once then twice.

"No." He finally says, "You are not well. Besides, you need to focus on University. Your exams are soon."

I march towards him and grab him by either arm.

"Jake, I got an A in my most recent exam. Plus, I have a tutor. I will be fine in my exams!" I tell him confidently, "And as for my mental health... I'm getting better."

I say the last part with a smile. It is true. It's almost as if since meeting Mr Anderson, I've healed. There is something about him which just soothes me. My brother's eye twitches, and I can almost hear the cogs turning in his head.

"Come on, Jake. You know it makes sense." I push. Finally, he relents, "Okay, but the minute I get a stable job, you quit. Deal?"

I take his outstretched hand with a wide smile.

"Deal." I agree before taking a step back, "let me get changed and then you can drive me down?"

"Sure." He nods before sinking back into the sofa. For the first time in a while, he visibly relaxes. I watch as he rolls his shoulders and clicks his neck. The tension washes off him for a minute.

I disappear quickly to find some more suitable clothes. After a quick dig down the boxes, I settle on some dark trousers with a pale blouse. I run my fingers through my hair to detangle the matted knots before stumbling back into the living room, trying to slot my black boots on in the meantime.

"Ready?" My brother asks without looking at me. He slouches over the ancient computer in the corner of the room and then double clicks. The equally old, and falling apart, printer roars to life. We wait patiently as it slowly churns out two pieces of paper. Jake grabs it before turning to face me. He thrusts the document in my hands.

"This is your CV, I found it in the google drive." He tells me. I peer down at the document I made a year ago. In the top right corner, a happier version of myself smiles back. Little did this girl know that a couple of months into the future, her life would fall apart.

"Let's go." My brother pulls me from my bitter thoughts. I carefully slot the CV into my bag before we exit the house.

The drive is fast and quiet. Neither my brother nor I dare to speak. A weird tension echoes through the air. It is almost like before, when he would drive me to my Sunday job in the bar and restaurant around the corner from our old house. For a moment, we can pretend like everything's fine. Like everything's as it was.

"Good luck." He tells me with a beam, "message me when you're done okay?"

"Will do." I place a fake smile to my lips. He gives me an awkward half hug before I jump out of the vehicle. Afraid I might change my mind if I wait too long, I race through The Bar's doors. A huge crowd greets me.

I squeeze to the front of the queue with lots of 'thank you' and 'sorry'. Behind the bar, two overworked students frantically make the drinks.

"Excuse me," I call over at them before placing my CV on the side. I nervously look between them and the CV.

"I'm looking for a job." I give them my best smile, "This is my resume."

The larger blonde lady scoffs as she tosses a cocktail shaker from one hand to the other.

"Ever worked behind a bar before?" She raises an eyebrow. With a small smile, I nod my head quickly.

"Yes, for two years." I tell her. The blonde lady pulls a face and smiles.

"Get behind the bar." She instructs before pouring the contents of the shakers into three separate glasses. My face pales.

"What? Right now?" I gawp at her.

"Do you want the job?" The blonde lady snaps. I race into action and slip through the wooden door to join them behind the bar. The crowd is huge now, and each person demands your attention. They wave credit cards in your face and shriek anything to get you to look at them.

"Um, next?" I say nervously, peering towards a scrawny looking boy. He thrusts a ten-pound note into my fingers.

"Two corona bottles." He barks. I nod and twist to face the huge bar. After a second of hesitation, I find the bottles in the bottom fridge.

"Want limes with that?" I raise an eyebrow up at him. He nods quickly so I get to work on finding the limes. With a satisfied smile, I turn and hand him both the bottles before walking towards the till. It is simple enough to understand and before I know it, I'm serving the next customer.

Slowly, the rush hour ends. The crowds of people all drop away from the bar to find places to sit and enjoy themselves. I wipe the layer of sweat from my forehead as I serve the last customer on my side of the bar.

"You're a natural." The blonde lady grins. She wipes her hands on the apron before sticking it out in front of me.

"My name is Amy, I'm the manager here." She smiles politely, "sorry if I was rude back there, it gets too overwhelming behind the bar."

"I understand." I respond with a bob of my head. She returns her gaze to the counters as she cleans up the mess we've all made, "So, I've seen your skills. Now I want to know your availability."

"Does that mean I have the job? You don't know anything about me!" I say the words before I snap my lips shut. *Why would I say such an off-putting thing!*

"Nobody ever tells the truth about their personality on the first shift. I will get to know the real you as you work. But now, I still want to know your availability." She raises an eyebrow at me. A huge smirk teases my lips,

"I can do weekends and whenever you need me on the weekday. Though I have University between one and four most days."

"Brilliant." She sighs, "I need an extra pair of hands around here. Everybody is dropping out, yet the crowds are multiplying."

She sticks her hand out to me again. Nervously, I take it.

"Welcome to the team." She beams.

# CHAPTER SEVENTEEN

## Willow's Pov:

Nervously, I peer down at the sheet of paper in my fingers. An address for *'Lively Green'* stares back up at me. Mr Anderson told me we were going to have our tutoring session in a different place today due to the lecture hall being booked out by another class. At first, I hadn't objected. However, staring up at the large tree before me, with the squirrels chattering down, my stomach twists nervously and I really wish I had objected.

The fresh grass fills my nostrils and makes me feel all happy inside. I lug my bag up the green, past the glistening lake, towards a bench. My lungs heave as I finally sit down. Around me, the scenery is tranquil. Everything is quiet, peaceful. I close my eyes and take another deep breath. It feels as though all my problems disappear.

"Willow?" Mr Anderson's voice pulls me from my relaxation. I readjust my position on the bench and allow him space to sit next to me.

"Hi." I answer sheepishly. My gaze casts around at the beautiful scenery. *Why would he take me here for our session?*

"Today, we are doing a descriptive task." He tells me with a small smile. His hand rests on my thigh and it makes me lose focus. The warm, possessive touch makes my heart flip. I gulp, "On what?"

"Look around you." He beams, "You will be describing what you see."

"Why here?" I ask before I can stop myself. I don't understand why he couldn't have shown me a picture of the scenery for me to describe. Why would he physically take me here during our tutoring sessions? He sighs and shuffles closer. His gorgeous scent makes me feel dizzy. I want to drink it all up and stay wrapped in those strong arms for the rest of my life.

"It's my place of solitude." He whispers, "When the world gets too much, this is where I go. And I want you to describe it. You have a talent for writing."

His eyes twinkle in the early morning sun. A slight breeze moves past us, and I shiver. Silently, I regret not bringing a thicker coat. With a smile, he pulls his jacket off. I watch in shock as he drapes it around my shoulders.

"You're going to get cold." I scold him before pulling the coat from my shoulders. He quickly protests and wraps me up again,

"I'd rather freeze to death than let you get cold."

As I try to calm my erratic heart, he shuffles beside me, and surprises me by brushing his fingers down my cheek. I swivel to stare up at him, caught by surprise, but his fingers don't recoil back. The pads of his fingers are rough against my soft skin, but it feels so *right.* Unable to speak suddenly, I stare into his gorgeous amber eyes as they flicker between mine. He's biting the inside of his cheek, like he wants to say something, and I can't help but reach forwards, to touch his own cheek. The bristle of his beard tickles against my hands as I trace the outline of his jaw with my index finger. Under the glare of the sun, his face is so painfully handsome that it steals my breath away.

"You are beautiful Willow." He says suddenly, completely taking me aback. My fingers freeze against his face as I digest these words.

*Me? Beautiful?* The words don't resonate. *He* is the beautiful one.

Strong, powerful, handsome. How does he find *me* beautiful –
broken, small me?

With a gulp, I pull my hand sharply away and fold them
anxiously in my lap. However, he tilts my head back towards
him.

"Willow," He says sternly. The sudden change in tone causes me
to meet his eye again. "Don't do that. Don't go into your head and
doubt my words. You *are* beautiful, you are the prettiest woman
I've ever met."

Now my cheeks are the colour of roses and I feel the shiver
shudder down my spine at his delicate words. Against my cheek,
his fingers continue to stroke my skin and subconsciously I
lean into them. My words feel like mush; if I speak, I'll surely
embarrass myself, so I stay quiet.

After a beat, he gently pulls me closer and my heart thumps hard
in my chest as he lowers his lips to mine. Electric travels down
my spine, causing every hair on my body to stand up right; his
lips are so soft and so *welcoming*, that I lose myself in them.

I don't remember when I moved my hands to his chest, but I
don't argue with it. With a small sigh, I grip his top tightly and
push further into him.

He moves his head, so my lips fall to his own lips too. My heart
flips in my chest when he parts his lips to deepen the kiss. I don't
know what it is about him, but one kiss has me ready to beg for
more. He is like my drug, and I desire much more. I want to ride
this high for the rest of my life, never sobering up until the day
my breath is stolen from my lungs. Mr Anderson is my new life
source.

"Willow." He growls into my lips. The noise sends vibrations
through me and makes me shiver. I clutch his shoulders as he
slides me onto his lap.

"Oh!" I gasp when I feel his hard member straining through
his trousers. A deep grumble leaves his lips as his hands fix

themselves onto my hips. He never stops kissing me, and I silently plead he never does. I choose his breath over oxygen any day of the week. One of his hands creep up under my top. His touch is cold, but it adds to my desire much more. Then, he twiddles my nipple. I gasp in shock and lurch forward.

"That's it." He whispers into my ear. The sound is animalistic, possessive. Then, his other hand trails down and into my leggings. Quickly, he slips under my underwear too.

"Mr Anderson!" I pant, "We can't. N-not here."

"Why not?" He says, planting a kiss on my neck. His fingers find my clit and he teases it slowly before quickening up. I squirm under his touch and desperately try to control my erratic breathing.

"Good girl." He says before nipping at my ear. His words only spur me on more. Before long, I am close on the edge. He overwhelms me with his lips on my neck, a finger on my nipple and then his other hand massaging my clit.

"Wait!" I hiss, pushing him back. I bite my lower lips nervously and look up at him through low eyes, "I want you inside of me."

He jolts backwards and stares at me with shock. The sensual attack on my body stops. Slowly, he shakes his head,

"No, I can't take your virginity. Not here, Willow."

"What better place?" I whisper with a small smile. I cast my eyes around. The only thing which accompanies us are the ducks and the gorgeous scenery. He bites his lower lip and considers my suggestion. He shakes his head once, then twice.

"No." He says, "Your first time should be with someone special. Just let me pleasure you until you find him."

I press my lips to his and kiss him passionately. He can't resist but kiss back.

"You are that special person." I whimper, "Please. I want you to take it."

He stares into my eyes, desperately searching to see whether I'm telling the truth. My fingers fumble with the zip on his trousers to sway his decision. Suddenly, he snaps. He can no longer hide the truth: he wants me, and I want him. You can't resist desire this strong.

"Fuck, Willow. You're going to be the death of me." He hisses before lifting me off him. I tremble with anticipation and the chill as I watch him unbuckle his trousers. Then he sits back down and pulls me towards him. Like a crazed animal, he rips through my leggings, making a huge hole. I gasp in shock, but my body reacts positively. He is incredibly sexy.

"Come here." He growls. I quickly obey and straddle him again. Now, I feel his huge member press against the thin material of my knickers through the hole in my leggings. His fingers jump down, and he pushes it aside. Then, he runs his cock through my wetness. I gasp in pleasure, "Mr Anderson!"

"That's it." He hums in approval. I squirm as he shakes his member against my clit. I feel like I could combust there and then.

"Please." I whimper desperately, "I want you inside of me!"

He wraps one arm around me and pulls me close. I feel him move his member lower.

"Are you sure, Willow? Once we do this, there is no going back." He tells me with big eyes, "Once we do this, you're mine forever. And I don't share."

His words make my stomach flip in my stomach. I couldn't imagine anything better. He brings me to life; he brings me pleasure wrapped in happiness. I nod frantically, "Yes! Yes, please make me yours!"

Suddenly, he plunges inside of me. I gasp in shock as the pain ripples through me. He steadies himself and holds me close. Our gaze meets and it feels like I'm falling into him. Slowly, the pain subsides. It's replaced with an unimaginable pleasure.

"Oh my God." I whimper. My legs begin to shake as he thrusts upwards. His hands hold my hips still as he starts to thrust faster and faster. Blissed out, my head lulls backwards. His grunts and groans only spur me on further.

"That's it, Willow." He encourages me. Then, one of his fingers jump to my clit. It's all too much. I jolt forward and grip onto his shoulders. He has me right on edge.

"Yes, good girl." He hisses, "cum for me. Cum all over me."

I quickly obey him. With two more thrusts, I fall over the edge. A scream of pleasure escapes my lips, but I quickly bite into his shoulder to stop the sound. My reaction pushes him over the edge. I shiver from my comedown as he empties himself inside of me. I can't move, my knees feel weak. All I can do is cling to him like there is no tomorrow. He does the same, wrapping his protective arms around me.

I am blissed out with joy. All my worries of jobs and delusions simply disappear into the background. I press my head against his chest and listen to his racing heartbeat. The sound soothes me. *He* soothes me.

# CHAPTER EIGHTEEN

## Mr Anderson's Pov:

"He's inside?" I frown at Olivia. She nods nervously and chews at her fingernails.

"Let's go then." I say, "What are we waiting for?"

"I'm anxious." She squeaks, casting her eyes towards the café across the road. Slowly, I nod my head in understanding. I'm nervous too. Inside that building is the man who is going to tell us what drug Emily is taking. As far as I'm concerned, she was completely pill free when we were married. What's changed?

"It's a step closer to the truth, Olivia." I try to reassure her, "After this meeting, hopefully things will become much clearer."

"You're right." She sighs before unbuckling her seatbelt, "Let's get this over and done with."

I follow her out the car and up to the café entrance. In the far corner, a skittish looking man hunches over. He shuffles uncomfortably in his seat and his eyes dart around nervously. It appears he is just as anxious as us.

"Mike Colwell?" I ask him as we approach. He nods quickly. Olivia gives me one last look before we take a seat in front of him.

At the sight of us, the man's eyes go wide like saucepans, as he glances between us. They settle on me, on how much taller I am than him, and he shrinks anxiously into his chair.

Pretending not to notice the motion, I take a seat in front of the man, folding my hands on the table between us. Olivia shoots me a look in the corner of my eye, but I am too busy studying the wimpy man in front of me to look back.

"So, what is it?" I demand. The man flinches, eyes darting between me and Olivia. He looks rough, unshaven and heavy bags under his eyes so large, I wonder if he's slept in the last week. Mentally, I scowl Olivia for letting this *thing* deal with an issue so important to me, but don't say anything, knowing it's our only chance. We cannot be caught searching for the answer ourselves. Digital footprints are far too dangerous when going against a force as destructive as my ex-wife.

"What's in the pill, Mike?" Olivia asks softly. At her voice, the man focuses entirely on her, shoulders sagging silently in comfort at the reassuring smile on her face.

"Ativan." He responds in a similar hushed tone. "It's used to treat all sort of things, like epilepsy, anxiety, insomnia … I can send you a list if you want it."

"Of course, we want it." I snap, and the man jumps, as if remembering my presence. With a sharp look in my direction, Olivia folds her hands out on the table, close to the man's.

"We would really appreciate a list." She corrects my sharp tone, sending him one of her intoxicating smiles, which the man falls for. His face softens as he looks at the thirty-year-old beside me. Out of the classroom, Olivia dresses differently but still holds the schoolgirl aura around her. Her red hair is loose around her shoulders, not back combed for once. She's gone easy with the makeup, sporting a pair of glasses and a soft shade of lipstick that looks completely different to the black or deep red one she normally wears to my lessons. She's dressed in a skin-tight turtleneck that compliments her curves, and mum jeans that catches the man's gaze whenever she crosses and uncrosses her long legs. The friendly adult look seems to work on the man in front of us – *Mike* – because when she takes his hands in hers and rubs it gently with her thumb, he doesn't recoil away. Gritting my teeth, I try not to punch the weak man in front of me as he smiles sheepishly back at my best friend.

"Are there any side effects to the pill?" She asks him gently. I stiffen beside her, shooting her a suspicious look. *What kind of question is that?*

However, before I can ask her what she's implying, the man responds.

"Again, there's a whole list. I'll email them." He whispers. At the googly eyes he sends Olivia, I lose my composure slightly, growing restless at these answerless questions.

"Is it addictive?" I spit.

"Yes, of course. Especially if it's taken with other things." Mike stammers. "Is there another medicine being taken at the same time as it?"

With a grunt, I sit back in my chair. *How the fuck would I know what else she's taking?* I go to say, but once again, I'm cut off.

"Yes." Olivia says quickly. "Let's say, I don't know, *hypothetically* … What would happen if it was paired with heroin…"

The breath catches in my throat as I swivel on my best friend.

"What?" I seethe. *What is she implying about my ex-wife? That she's an epileptic drug addict?*

However, Olivia doesn't look at me, eyes square on Mike. Her face has gone slightly white; her gaze slightly wider as if she's afraid of what I'm about to say.

My heartbeat is in my ears as I stare at the woman beside me. Blood boiling, palms sweaty, head spinning. From beside us, Mike is talking but it's hard to focus.

"Perhaps. There will be sweating, confusion, aches, pains

maybe." Mike frowns, wrinkling his nose as he thinks. "I'm not sure completely. Lots of things could happen."

"Oh." Olivia releases his hands and sits back in his seat. At her absence, the man grows unsettled again, nervously glancing between the two of us.

"Is that it? Can I go now?" Mike whimpers. However, Olivia isn't looking at him anymore. She stares at the table before her, deep in thought, wrinkles creasing her forehead. My mouth is dry as I wave a hand at the man in front of us.

"Get out of my sight." I grunt. Pathetically, the man scrambles to his feet and all but runs to the exit. I watch him go as my mind scrambles to comprehend what's going on. After a long pause, I turn on Olivia.

"So, do you want to tell me what all of that was about?" I snarl. "When were you going to tell me about the heroin?"

Her face blanks momentarily, for once she is speechless – a very uncharacterised trait of Liv.

Finally, she swallows hard.

"I think … I think Emily was drugging you …"

The world comes screeching to a halt. My voice is so loud it makes my head ring as I gasp, *"What!?"*

Around us, people glance in our direction but I am too taken aback to care. The world is spinning around me as I desperately try to process this piece of information. My skin crawls at such a *stupid accusation*, but my heart races at the fear it could be true.

"Don't be stupid, Liv." I hear myself snap over the blood rushing past my ears. "I think I would know if my wife was drugging me!"

"Really?" She whirls on me, eyes narrowed and suddenly so angry. The change in her personality takes me by surprise. "Would you really know, Liam? Huh? Tell me then, why don't you like coffee anymore?"

I falter. *When did Liv notice I hated coffee?*

Baffled, I stammer to try and get the words out of my dry mouth.

"Because – because nobody makes it like she did. It's … bitter. I don't like the taste." I finally get out. Her eyes are so cold it makes me shiver; she is glaring at me like she wants a hole to burn into my face.

"Bullshit." She laughs spitefully. "You don't like coffee because she drugged it to make it taste better. You've told me yourself before, when you used to wake up, you'd be so stiff and in pain. Then your *beautiful, amazing, lovely wife* would bring you a steaming cup of coffee and suddenly you'd feel better!"

The way she spits the words make me flinch, but I try not to cower under her menacing gaze. My mind struggles to keep up with everything she is saying, I hold a hand up to silence her as a piercing pain starts to spread across my brain.

"Wait, I don't – "

However, Olivia keeps talking. "She made you associate her with the drugs in the coffee. Made you *addicted* to her so you'd never leave, Liam!" Her voice is shrill, making the pain in my head worse. "Do you remember how you were when she left, huh? The sweats? The anxiety? The depression? It was *withdrawal* symptoms, not heartbreak!"

"Hold on, Liv." I snap, placing my head in my hands. "You are going too quick. I can't keep up."

My whole body is shivering with adrenaline as I gasp in stale air. Around me, people blur as I focus on trying to calm down, but it's impossible.

"It doesn't make sense." I can hear myself mumbling, however my lips are so numb I don't realise I've said anything until I can hear it echoing around. "Why would she do that? Why … why would she leave me then?"

Beside me, Olivia bristles

"I don't know Liam." She huffs. "Why did that bitch do anything? Why would she take my husband? Why would she cheat? Why would she leave town suddenly and then return months later? The bitch is *psycho*! It's not out of character for her, is it?" Olivia hisses. A short silence drifts between us. I feel sick.

"She liked attention. She liked feeling wanted." I mutter, "So why would she leave me? I still don't understand. If I was hooked on every word, why find someone else?"

"Maybe she grew bored?" Olivia spits the harsh truth.

"Who did she find instead, Liv? Why wouldn't she just break up with me normally? Why flee the town for months only to return later and not mention anything to anyone?" I ramble on.

"I don't know, Liam!" She bursts out in frustration, "All we know is that she might be drugging somebody else now. But who? Which unlucky fellow is being drained as we speak?"

Shit. She's right.

The world is moving unnaturally quick around me as I lay my head down on the table. Bile burns at the back of my throat as the pain in my head causes my eyes to ache. Everything is so confusing; I am *so* confused.

Beside me, Olivia starts to calm herself down, realising the mess of emotions I am in. Her heavy breathing is contrasting my short shallow ones; my mind is so messy I can't work out which one of us moves first, but one of us does. She reaches out to touch my arm and I spring from my seat like I've been burnt.

Without another look at her, I grasp my coat on the back of my chair and storm towards the exit. Adrenaline coursing through my veins, my body has a mind of its own. My legs automatically move me towards my car, but instead of getting it, they carry me past, further down the road. Above, the clouds rumble as fat raindrops start to fall.

However, I pay them no notice.

I can't just sit and wonder why anymore - I need answers. I need … I need that bitch *dead*.

*  *  *

**WILLOW'S POV:**

"Can you pass me that lime?" Amy strains to reach the fruit on the side. I push it towards her and continue pouring the beer.

"Cheers." She says before sliding the wedge into a bottle. She takes the money off the customer and passes him the bottled drink, alongside the glass I just poured. With a nod of his head, the customer disappears to find a seat.

"Right." Amy sighs, checking her watch, "That is the big rush done. I'm going to go on my break for fifteen minutes. Are you okay here alone?"

"Yeah, sure." I smile politely. It's been a couple shifts now, so I am confident where everything is. Besides, it will be nice to be alone behind the bar. Amy is lovely and all, but it is suffocating having to work with your manager. It feels like everything you do is actually wrong. I gulp down my water and refill it. It is exhausting behind the bar, especially during happy hour.

"Perfect." Amy beams before undoing her apron. She hangs it on a bottle on the shelf before disappearing out into the back room, where all the storage is.

Before I get a chance to breathe at the absence of my boss, a voice startles me.

"Can I have an expresso martini?" A female voice gets my attention. I look at the beautiful blonde. Her bright red lips sparkle with some clear coating on the top. She has long lashes and dark blush on her tan skin. Something within me stirs. She seems familiar.

"Please?" The woman adds, pulling me from my thoughts.

"Course." I say with a smile before gathering my ingredients. I turn my back to grab the shaker and I mix everything together with ice. It makes a satisfying noise as I shake it as hard as I can. I give the customer a polite smile. She quickly returns the smile before looking away. With one hand, I bash the shaker against the table to make it open easier, and with the other I grab a glass. Expertly, I pour the beautiful dark liquid into the glass before placing three coffee beans in a triangle on top.

"That will be six pounds fifty, please." I tell the woman, plugging it into the till. She pulls out her yellow purse and pays in coins. I offer her the glass and she quickly disappears, not even waiting for her change. With a smile, I pop the extra two quid into the tip jar.

The bar is slowly emptying as the night closes up. I take the moment to take another drink. The liquid cools my stomach and quenches my thirst.

Another customer returns to the bar. I make quick work serving them. And then another comes up.

As I go to collect the empty glasses beside me, my hand misses, and knocks one straight onto the floor. Frowning, I glance down at the shards, but I don't have time to wonder how I knocked it over. My head is going foggy, and my throat is closing up. Somewhere nearby, a customer gets to their feet.

"Hey, are you okay?" Their words get lost in my head as I stagger to the side. Around me, the world is spinning faster and faster. I can't keep up.

*What is happening?*

With a gasp, I try to reach out for the bar to steady myself, but it shifts under my reach. I stumble forwards, and suddenly, I'm falling. As I tumble to the ground, the floor morphs before my very own horrified eyes. Red. Orange. Yellow. Pink. Swirls of bright, captivating colours twist and twirl into pretty patterns, as if I'm falling through dimensions. My eyes flutter open and shut. Each time I open them, my swirly portal in front of my eyes switches colours. And then suddenly, it all goes black.

# CHAPTER NINETEEN

## Willow's Pov:

"How is it going, Willow?" Doctor Jane enters the room. She rubs some sort of gel into her hands as she takes a seat at her usual desk. Quickly, she grabs my file before turning to face me. Her lips are pulled into a straight line. Nervously, I pull my legs to my chest and rest my chin on my knees. I have no memory of getting here. One minute I was at work, the next, I'm sitting in this seat.

"Good." I lie.

"That's not what it looks like." She sighs, dropping the clipboard in her lap. Slowly, she wheels closer to me, "Tell me again what happened at work."

"I was making a drink and then I passed out. I don't remember anything else." I recite my memory, but it is clearly not the answer she wants. She shakes her head and tuts at me, "No, Willow. You attacked someone. Do you remember who?"

"Huh?" I gasp, "I didn't attack anyone!"

"How would you know if you say you don't remember?" She asks sternly. My mouth opens and closes like a fish.

"You have to believe me." I tell her slowly, "I don't think I attacked anyone."

"CCTV shows you leaping over the bar and attacking a customer." Doctor Jane sighs before looking down at the scratches on my body. I stare at the small traces of blood and the breath catches in my lungs.

"No." I whisper, the tears stinging my eyes, "I couldn't have."

A long silence prevails between us before she releases a long breath.

"I'm sorry, Willow, but I do not feel comfortable letting you leave today's session." She says, standing up from the chair. My eyebrows burrow together. *What does she mean by that?*

"For that reason, you will be going to a facility to get you specialised help..." She begins as she picks up the phone on the desk. I leap to my feet.

"No!" I wail, "No, don't do that, please!"

My thoughts race one hundred miles an hour. *Surely, she can't send me away without consent?*

"Jake won't have it! He needs me, I'm the only one with a job!" I ramble to my doctor. She places the phone beneath her chin and scowls at me.

"You mean the job you just lost?" She frowns, "And besides, Jake agrees with me."

"You spoke to my brother?" I say quietly. A betrayal ripples through me. *Did my brother actually agree to send me away? Does he think I am a burden? Am I dragging him down?*

"Yes, please send security upstairs to room 5a. Thank you." Doctor Jane says down the phone before hanging up. She peers at me with sympathetic eyes.

"I'm sorry, Willow. But you need a place where you can be monitored twenty-four hours a day." She scowls.

"No!" I beg, falling to my knees.

I pull at her trousers and sob, "Don't make me go! I don't want to be locked up. Give me more pills! I will take them all, I swear!"

"Willow, we can continue making progress whilst you're in that facility. Trust me, it's what is best for you right now." She says as she awkwardly pats my head.

Suddenly, the door slams open, and all hope drains from me. On the other side of the room, two paramedics enter, eyes fixed on me. Frightened, I back up and hold my hands up.

"No, please!" I whimper.

"Willow, don't make this harder than it needs to be." Doctor Jane scolds me as the paramedics close in. I close my eyes and try to steady my breathing. They take the opportunity to grab me by either arm. I scream out in misery as they drag me from the room. No matter how hard I buck my body against them, they are much stronger and pull me out of the building as if I weight nothing.

Suddenly, time speeds up again. Everything feels dizzy and the light is too bright. When it finally calms down, I'm sitting in a chair with my brother opposite. He stares down at the table numbly.

"Jake?" I squeak. His eyes shoot up and he reaches out for me. I try to hold his hand, but both my arms are chained to the chair. The panic takes a hold of me, and I try to thrust away.

"No, Willow! Calm down." He scolds me. The tears flow down my face. I don't even care for the dozens of other people in the room, all facing their crazy loved ones.

"What have you done, Jake?" I shriek, "Why would you send me here?"

The tears flow hard and fast down my face. I choke on the sobs. I feel the snot drip down my face, but I don't care. How could he? My own brother sent me away!

Panicked, my gaze flits around the room. No more than two meters away, another girl with her arms chained behind her back sits talking to somebody else. Beside her, another pair. As my eyes frightenedly flicker around the room, the realisation dawns on me. *I'm in a mental ward.*

"You need this place." He tells me miserably, "Willow, you're very sick."

"I am not!" I hiss, "I have it all under control. Just get me out of here, please."

"Ah, she's awake." Doctor Jane's voice echoes through the room. My tear-stricken face shoots up to her. Quickly, she drags a chair from the other corner of the room and sets herself up next to my brother. My heart constricts in agony as I look between them.

"What is happening?" I whimper desperately.

"You're too sick to be in your brother's care." Doctor Jane tells me. I refuse to look at Jake when I answer, "How long am I here for?"

"Until you're better." She sighs. A scoff falls past my lips. Those three words have damned me for life. I have been struggling with my mental health since I was ten. It has been getting worse and worse. I will never get better. And now I will never be free.

"But I have University." I tell her sternly, "I have exams to sit."

Doctor Jane and Jake exchange a nervous glance. I feel my body freeze as a cold chill shivers through me.

"About that, Willow." My brother whispers. His voice is hoarse, and I can almost hear the lump in his throat, "Where have you been going to these last couple weeks?"

My eyebrows burrow together on my forehead.

"What do you mean? I've been at University." I tell him in confusion. A tear slips down his face and this time, he can't bring himself to look at me. Frightened, I look to my doctor.

"Willow, I've checked attendance records. You haven't shown up to a single lecture nor a revision session." She tells me sternly, "Where have you been?"

It feels as though the world has stopped around me. My head cocks to the side and my eye twitches as another tear slips down my face.

"I've been at University." I tell her slowly. What part of that does she not understand? Where was she getting her information from? She can go and ask Mr Anderson herself and he will tell her I've been there every day.

"Not according to your professor." Jake whispers, eyes still fixed on the table.

"Mr Anderson?" I raise an eyebrow in confusion, "Yes, I've been to almost every session and revision session!"

"No, Willow." Doctor Jane pulls my attention towards her, "I have spoken to him. He says you haven't. Other students don't recognise your picture either."

"What?" I squeak, "That can't be. Check with Dylan and Olivia!"

My doctor and brother exchange another nervous look.

"What?" I scoff in anger, "You're not going to tell me I'm making them all up, are you?"

My disgusted humour for the situation slowly disappears when neither my Jake nor Doctor Jane smile. This stills me for good. More tears slip down my cheeks. The salty taste makes me feel even more sick.

"Right?" I whisper. The sound is small, desperate. I need them to tell me I'm not crazy. I know I have been interacting with real people these past few weeks. I don't understand why they won't believe me.

"No, Willow. They are not real people." Doctor Jane tells me sensitively, "Well, Dylan is. But he reckons he has never met you before."

"That's ridiculous. And that is only because I didn't kiss him!" I blurt out and then stop myself. I sound ridiculous. My brother shakes his head as if he is trying to shake what is happening out of his memory.

"You have to believe me." I tell them both sternly, "I am not being delusional this time, I swear!"

"Willow you are very sick. More so than what we thought beforehand." Doctor Jane speaks for them both.

"This is my fault." My brother whispers weakly. I scowl, "What? How is it your fault, Jake?"

"I pushed you too hard. To return to university, to get a job. You've snapped." He confesses. Doctor Jane puts an arm around my brother. Frantically, I look between the two of them.

"Stop it! I haven't snapped. Don't talk about me like that. I am perfectly sane." I panic, "Doctor I have been taking your pills every day, doing the breathing exercises. Trust me, they are real people!"

My head snaps towards my brother, "Jake, you saw Mr Anderson that day at the doctors, right?"

"No, Willow, I didn't." He whispers. My heart skips a beat in my chest.

"What about when you've dropped me off at the pub?" I try again desperately. He shakes his head again.

"Willow, I've never met any of these people."

"That proves nothing!" I squeak defensively, "You haven't met a lot of people and yet you know they exist! The Queen, for example!"

"You're becoming hysterical." Doctor Jane hushes me when more eyes turn our way, "And Willow the Queen has documented evidence of her existence. Like pictures and millions of people have seen her."

I purse my lips and think rapidly. What could I say to prove that they all exist? That I've done sexual things with Mr Anderson? No, they wouldn't believe that.

"What does Mr Anderson look like?" I turn to Doctor Jane quickly. I refuse to believe that he doesn't exist. But then the other option is that he is actively rejecting me. I don't know which one is worse.

"I, uh…" Doctor Jane stumbles over her words, "Willow, please don't fight us on this one. You have imagined him."

"Does he have a scar on his thumb?" I blurt, "He has dark eyes, dark hair. He is tall, handsome and…"

"Willow, stop!" My brother snaps as he throws his fist into the table. I jolt and snap my lips shut.

"Just stop talking. You're embarrassing yourself." He hisses, "Just think for one second. Who is more likely to be right? Me and your Doctor, amongst university records, or you?"

I don't answer him. I can't answer him. He's right.

My heart drops in my chest.

"We will talk through some of these delusions during our therapy sessions, Willow." Doctor Jane tells me with a sad smile, "But for now, you need to rest. Get some sleep. We will catch up tomorrow."

"What? No. Don't leave just yet." I cry out as my brother gets up to leave. My handcuffs force me to stay still. It feels as though my heart is caving in as my brother sobs.

"You must believe me." I call out to him, "Jake please. I swear… Check CCTV of the bar! It shows Olivia there with me!"

"And what would you have me say to the business where you have attacked one of their customers and ruined their reputation? It's not going to happen, Willow." He snaps.

"Then check the cameras outside. Just please…" I start but yet again he cuts me off.

"Stop!" He barks, stumbling backwards. His fingers tug at his hair in distress.

"I will call you in the week." He says numbly before fleeing the room. Everything hurts as I watch my doctor chase after him.

Slowly, I scan the room. Everyone in orange looks crazy. Some bark, some stare into nothingness and others laugh manically. The noises are too much. They are too overbearing. Everyone here is fucking crazy. And now I'm one of them!

# CHAPTER TWENTY

## Willow's Pov:

*Smoke fills my lungs. It startles me awake. The black mist around me makes me splutter and cough. I throw my shirt to my mouth for cover and stumble out the door. Around me the house roars with flames. I feel the heat lick my skin and I profusely sweat. I stumble out the room and stare up at the stairs which leads to my parents' floor.*

*"Mum? Dad?" I shriek but the howls of the fire quickly remove my voice. I try again and again to no avail. My body forces me forward up the stairs to check on them but a beam from the ceiling falls down. It roars with fire and misses me by inches. I stumble backwards, looking desperately for my parents. Have they escaped the burning house yet?*

*"Mum! Dad!" I howl.*

*"We're here!" A voice calls behind me. I spin around. My mum stands there, in her brilliant yellow dress. She stands in the fire, unflinching. Her eyes are cold and hard as she watches me. Beside her, my father wraps an arm around her shoulders.*

*"What are you doing?" I hiss as the flames engulf them. Both of them glare at me with a burning hatred.*

*"You did this." My dad spits, "You killed us."*

*I fall to my feet and grip at my hair. No! I won't let them taunt me like this. These nightmares have to stop at some point. I scream and scream to drown out my parents' taunting words. They spit unimaginable insults at me.*

*"Willow?" A voice cries out. It is familiar. My head shoots upwards and Mr Anderson is here. However, he wears an equally devilish look. He has no eyeballs, they have melted out, and his skin is slowly tarring from the fire. Olivia steps in beside him. All of her hair is gone, and half her face has peeled off. Then Mr Fluffy appears in my nightmare too. It shrieks and cries as it burns in a smaller fire.*

*"No!" I howl, "Stop it! Stop it!"*

*The four of them and the cat shuffle together. They each chant something in a different language. I can't understand it. I don't want to understand it. It gets louder and louder until it successfully echoes over the fire.*

*"Stop!" I cry, "Please, please I'm sorry. You are not real! This isn't real!"*

*The tears won't fall, the scorching fire evaporates them before they can expose themselves. Mr Anderson takes a step towards me. His hands reach out as if they are going to wrap around my neck. Like my father used to, Mr Anderson is going to strangle me. However, the touch is soft, forgiving.*

*"Wake up." He whispers. Around us, the house collapses in on itself. I don't want to leave. I deserve to die with the rest of my friends and family.*

*"Wake up, Willow!" He yells louder this time. The noise sends shivers all through me.*

Suddenly, I shoot up in the bed. My hands jump out to steady myself and instead of my usual warm blanket, there is scratchy rough sheets. Distressed, I sink my nails into the sheets. They rip. *Suicide proof.*

"Checks." A voice comes from behind the door. Slowly it opens and a nurse with a white, triangle hat steps into the room. In the dull stream of light coming from the corridor, her brown hair contrasts against her pale skin and light eyes. She is a very pretty woman.

"Oh, you're awake." She says, surprised. My heart still pounds frantically. The lady enters the room and flicks the light on. It reveals a simple room with just a bed and a window.

A scratchy blue dress hangs loosely from my body. I move my hand to my head to wipe the sweat, but I'm stopped. This arm is connected to a bunch of wires. My other wrist is hand cuffed to the bed.

"This isn't necessary." I whimper, referring to the chains. The lady offers me a sad smile as she checks on the large monitor above the bed. She clicks a couple buttons.

"It was for your safety, and ours." She answers with kind eyes, "You seem calmer now though. Let me take them off, but if you try anything funny, we will have to cuff you again. Is that clear, Willow?" Her tone is sweet, but authoritative, like a motherly figure, and I warm to her. Obediently, I nod my head and she makes quick work of freeing my hand. I rub the sore part on my wrist protectively.

With a sigh, the nurse looks at the watch on her wrist and sighs, "It's a bit early, but I suppose you could come to breakfast if you want to get out of this room? Some other patients will be there too."

The gulp gets caught in my throat. *Patients.* I am just another mental case like them. Without waiting for my reply, the nurse fiddles with my wires and the monitor next to my bed. I nod my head anyways to confirm that I want to leave this nightmarish room. But I nod too quickly. It makes me feel dizzy and a flood of nausea rushes through me.

In the corner of the room, my mum suddenly appears. She leans against the wall, face pulled into a permanent frown as she watches me. At first, she seems frustrated as her arms are folded tightly across her chest, and then an alarmed look strikes her. Her eyes are frantic and shooting everywhere, and I watch, in shock, as her chest rises when she inhales a huge gust of air, before opening her lips wide as if she is screaming. But the sound doesn't follow. She lunges forward but an invisible field keeps her trapped against the wall. She shrieks again, still soundless.

"You'll feel a little funny all day." The nurse tells me, "You were heavily sedated last night."

"I was?" I whisper.

The nurse's lips pull together in a straight line. She nods her head quickly, "Yes, you quickly became violent after being left alone for a while."

"I did?" I squeak in despair. *Why didn't I remember this? What is happening to me?*

"Unfortunately." The nurse nods her head. She finishes up pulling the wires out of my veins. I flinch as it stings. Then, she stands backwards.

"What about these?" I say, holding my hands up. A large needle remains in both. On the surface, a tube with a plug in it remained.

"Do not touch those. We keep them in, in case of emergency and we need to drug you up again." She says. A shiver wracks through my body.

"Isn't this dangerous?" I frown, "I could tear through my skin?"

"That's what the tape is for." She explains. Numbly, I look down at the flimsy bit of tape. It uneases me. In case of a break down, or an attack, they could quite easily be ripped from my body.

"Again, it's just for today, dear." She says kindly. Then, she offers a hand to me. Hesitantly, I take it and stand to my feet. The dress drops below my knees.

"Let's go and get breakfast, shall we?" She tells me before leading me out of the room. I wince and groan as my achy body moves. It feels as though I have just run a marathon. I almost beg her to climb back into bed. But I don't. I need to escape my mother's miserable face.

Slowly, she leads me down winding hallways. Despite the lack of windows, it is surprisingly bright. Each stain free wall reflects the light brighter and brighter until it gives you a headache. The smell of ammonia wafts around too. I try not to think about people wetting themselves on these very floors as we take another left and then right. The nurse nods politely towards another nurse as he walks past. His eyebrows burrow together when they spot me, but he masks it quickly and continues on past.

"Oh, I'm Nurse Amori, by the way." The brown-haired nurse smiles around at me. I don't answer her.

Finally, we arrive at a large canteen. This room is huge and packed with tables and chairs, the kind which are attached to each other by a metal pole. The smell of warm porridge fills my nose, but it isn't a good smell. It's almost like hot porridge gone stale. I turn my nose up and follow Nurse Amori to the far side of the room, towards the serving counter. A couple people wearing hair nets stand behind the counter. They each grip onto a spoon, ready to serve up breakfast.

"Mornin' Amori." One of them says. This girl has blotchy skin and piercing eyes. Her hair is patchy, like red dye slowly growing out, and she wears clothes way too loose for her thin body.

"Good morning, Carly." She responds politely before scrunching her face up at the food, "Is it just porridge today?"

"Afraid so." Carly shrugs her shoulders. Nurse Amori gestures towards me, and Carly quickly serves up a bowl of watery oats. She trembles slightly, her bamboo like arms looking like sticks in the wind. Nurse Amori picks up on it too.

"Have you eaten this morning?" She frowns. Carly plasters a quick smile to her lips and nods frantically, "Course I have."

Nurse Amori holds her gaze a little longer. It's clear that they both know she is lying, but it's just a wait of who is first to snap.

"No, she aint!" A larger lady beside her blurts, "She aint! She aint! She aint!"

163

"Zip it, Cow!" Carly seethes. The lady beside her starts jumping up and down, faster and faster. I watch in repulsion as she works up a sweat next to the food.

"Thank you, Cow." Nurse Amori raises a hand to signal her to calm down. My face contorts. *Is this Lady's name really Cow?* I thought it was an insult!

"She aint though, miss. I'm tellin' ya now, she aint touched food for..." Cow begins but is cut off as Carly leaps towards her.

"Shut up, snitch!" She shrieks. They both tumble to the ground as they throw limbs into each other's body's. Nurse Amori breaks into action, shrieking things into her walkie talky. Mortified, I slowly stumble backwards. The two fighting disappear out of sight behind the counter, but their cries of pain and anger still echo around this hollow room.

I cast my eyes around and see a steady stream of crazy people entering the hall. Quickly, I take my place at a far table away from all the mess. My stomach growls but I dare not touch the watery shit in a bowl. Perhaps that's why Carly won't eat; and if the person in the kitchen will not eat her own food, what chance does the rest of us have?

A leggy brunette enters the room. She has hoisted her blue dress to reveal her tanned thighs and has somehow hitched it at the back. Long flowing hair cascades around her waist, it dances as she advances further into the room. Her gaze spots the commotion, and she freezes. Bitterly, she folds her arms and scowls.

"It's seven in the fucking morning!" She suddenly shrieks. All eyes are on her. Some people in the room jolt and scurry away. Even the people fighting stop their attack. They both shoot to their feet and look at this lady guiltily.

"Thank you, Miss Rover." Nurse Amori says bitterly, "But we had it. No need to swear."

Wide eyed, I look between Nurse Amori and the other beautiful lady whose lips pull into a grim line. Something in her eyes twinkle mischievously. I watch her jaw clench, and for a second, it looks as if a second fight of the day is going to break out. Then, Miss Rover averts her attention. She scans the room before settling on me.

Though she doesn't say anything, her lips part and something quizzical dances around her expression. I tear my gaze towards the table and keep my head low. I don't need to get on the wrong side of anyone, especially when they are all fucking crazy. In the distance, a female voice starts barking. It is joined by a couple others followed by an awful cackling. I throw my hands over my head and glare at the table bitterly.

Being stuck in that shitty room, with my mother seems like a better option than hanging out with the Crazies.

# CHAPTER TWENTY-ONE

## Jake's Pov:

**I** struggle to put the key in the door as I balance all the shopping in my arms. I misplace my footing and stumble forward into the door. To my surprise, it is open. Warily, I enter my house and kick the door shut. Then I quickly put my bags on the sofa. Even though this is an old house with creaky, unreliable doors, I should check that I'm alone. I throw my coat off to give me more movement and peer around my kitchen.

Then, I return to the hallway and tip toe down. My door is locked from earlier, so I don't bother checking there. Instead, I head towards Willow's room. Her door is slightly open and a cold chill seeps through the gap. For a second, I think I can hear panting, but it quickly disappears the closer I get. My eyes play tricks on me as a shadow races past in her room.

Violently, I kick the door open and jump inside, ready to take on the intruder. However, as I stumble in, I'm greeted by nothing. Only an open window and her textbooks flapping around in the wind. Shakily, I take a deep breath before shutting the window. I slowly start to clean up Willow's room. The guilt takes hold of me.

She should be here, with me. Not in that looney bin. But what can you do when your own blood turns even more psychotic? I can deal with the anxiety and delusions. Even the depression to some point. But her physically attacking people? That's not on. Selfishly, I wasn't concerned about the community or her victims. I was more worried about her lashing out at the wrong person. Someone who could press charges. And then Willow would spend a lot more time in prison than a mental hospital. It is just better this way. She'll be out before she even knows it.

Suddenly, there is a fumbling at the door. I jolt and spin around defensively. *Who could that be?*

Nervously, I approach the door. We do not have a keyhole so I cannot see who it is beforehand. It shakes as someone tries to unlock it. With a regulating breath, I open the door slightly and stick my head around.

"Hello?" I frown. A dark-haired beauty stairs back at me. She has wide, gentle eyes and a shocked look on her face.

"Oh, sorry!" She squeaks, "I thought this was my new apartment!"

I cautiously open my door a bit wider and spot all her suitcases.

"Is this 33-crescent drive?" She scowls, fumbling with a piece of paper. I pull the door open and go to point to our marker. To my surprise, it has worn away.

"I'm afraid not, this is 32. You're next door." I say, turning my attention back to her. She nervously bites her lower lip and peers round at the flat next to us. It is missing a door and the windows have been smashed in. When Willow and I arrived, there were rumours that there was a gang living in this row of flats. Apparently one day, the rival gang showed up and shot everybody dead. For my own sanity, I like to pretend it is just a rumour. There is rarely any truth behind rumours.

"Oh." She squeaks, taking a step back. She struggles to yank all her suitcases towards the door.

"Here," I offer, grabbing one, "Let me help you out."

"Really?" She beams, "That would be great thank you! I have a couple more bags in my car. I don't have much stuff, but I did a food shop on my way here."

I smile at her as she fumbles around nervously. She is very sweet looking with her small, freckled face. I wheel two suitcases into her flat. The layout is exactly the same as ours. Only, all her walls are rotting, and the smell of damp and mould is overbearing.

"Home sweet home." She mutters bitterly. I rest the suitcases against the least rotten wall and turn to face her. She is wearing a lacey blouse with a long, dark pencil suit. Under her arm is an expensive looking jacket. She looks too put together to be living in a place like this!

"It is just temporary." She sighs, reading my contorted face, "Hopefully a couple of weeks max and then I'm gone."

"Why?" I frown. Her lips pull into a straight line as she looks at me. A frightened look skitters across her face, but she quickly averts her eyes to avoid me seeing. After a short pause, she clears her throat and changes topic, "Could you help me with my shopping downstairs?"

"Sure." I smile. Her face lights up as she leads the way. We make quick work of unloading the rest of her car. She really wasn't kidding; she has barely anything!

I lug the last bag in through the doors and place them on the kitchen counter. Slowly, I turn around to her. She fumbles down one of her suitcases and slowly starts unpacking.

"I'll leave you to unpack then." I clasp my hands together. Frightened, her eyes shoot up.

"No!" She squeaks. I frown but she quickly corrects herself, "I mean, yes, sorry. You're probably very busy and I shouldn't take up anymore of your time. You've been great, thank you."

I don't move to leave. Instead, I look as she anxiously fumbles over her words. Then she stumbles towards her shopping bag and pulls out a bottle of wine. She thrusts it into my hands.

"To say thank you for helping me." She smiles up at me. I don't know why but something in my stomach flips. Her beautiful, big eyes sparkle when she beams. It is such a sight.

"Perhaps you could come over and help me drink it at some point?" I ask her before I could stop myself. She winces and for a moment, I think I've pushed too far. She is clearly running from something, living in these awful conditions. I don't want to pressure her into anything else.

"How about now?" She offers.

"Do you not have to unpack?" I raise an eyebrow up at her. She scoffs and shakes her head, "This can wait. It'll be nice to actually hang out with somebody."

"We can go to my place?" I say, looking at her mouldy sofa. There is some sort of red stain on it, and I really don't want to spend the night sitting on someone's blood.

"Sure." She smiles before following me next door.

I head to the cupboard and pull out two glasses. She moves my bags to the counter before taking a seat. Quickly, she slips out of her heels and makes herself at home. I am almost grateful for the universe introducing me to her. It will be lonely around here without Willow. I have never lived alone, I never wanted to. And now I have a neighbour who I could potentially hang out with. Just having another friendly face around the block is enough.

"So, what brings you to sunny Crescent Drive?" I smirk as I pour out the red wine. She giggles at my sarcasm and then sighs. Lifting an eyebrow, I pass her the glass and she gulps it down. After she finishes the glass, she wipes her lips with the back of her hand and gives me a sad smile.

"I'm running away from my boyfriend's house."

"Why?" I find myself asking the stupid question. She stiffens and stares down at her empty glass. Common sense takes a hold of me, "Sorry, I shouldn't pry. It's none of my business."

"No, no. it's fine." She smiles at me, placing a small hand over mine. The touch is soft and warm.

"He was a bad man. Always in trouble with money sharks. And quite heavy handed too." She whispers. My heart constricts and for some reason I long to protect this woman. She shuffles closer as a breeze rocks through the flat. I wrap an arm around her. It feels normal, as though we've been close for years, not just hours.

"I had to get out of there. He doesn't know where I am." She explains. Her eyes water as she retells her story. I squeeze her reassuringly.

"You're so brave." I tell her quietly.

"And now I don't even have a door." She scoffs, throwing a hand to her head, "That's clever, isn't it?"

"I will always listen out for you. Or you could always stay here for the first couple days until you get a door?" I suggest.

"Do you have the space?" She frowns before shaking her head quickly, "No, no, I can't ask that of you. You're too generous."

"Honestly, It will be my pleasure." I tell her, "My sister has..." I hesitate, "gone on holiday for a little bit. So, her room is available."

I don't know why I lie to her. Perhaps it might be humiliation that I've failed Willow? Or maybe it's something worse: *am I embarrassed of her?*

For a long moment, she smiles at me, and her eyes do all the talking. She bobs her head gratefully and pours herself more wine. Then, her eyes round in shock.

"Oh, how silly of me!" She blurts, "My name is Alice."

She holds a hand out to me. I quickly take it with a small smile, "I'm Jake."

"Jake." She tests my name out on her lips. It is a beautiful sound and makes me feel all warm inside. Slowly, she brings the glass to her mouth and takes a sip. I don't miss her tongue shooting out to lick up all the wine on her lips. Quickly, I avert my eyes. I can't let my thoughts get the better of me. This girl is in danger, and she just needs a friend right now.

"Want more wine?" Alice raises an eyebrow. Before I can answer, she is already refilling my glass. I thank her and take another drink. Suddenly, my phone rings. I startle to my feet and fumble around for it.

"Oh!" She jolts in shock, grabbing her chest protectively.

"Sorry." I say sheepishly before looking down at my phone, "It is my sister. I must take this."

"No worries," She says, holding her hands up, "I'll go get ready for bed. And then if it's okay with you, I'll come back later and take you up on that offer of a spare bed?"

"Sure." I tell her, my heart leaping in my chest. She bobs her head politely before exiting the room. I catch the way her hips sway as she walks away from me, and it makes something tingle in my chest.

The ringing of the phone pulls me from my thoughts.

"Willow?" I breathe out panickily. *What has gone wrong? Is she okay? Has some crazy person hurt her?*

"Jake? Jake? Can you hear me?" She calls out.

"Yes, I can hear you. Can you hear me?"

On the other end of the phone, she sighs. I hear the slight tremble in her voice.

"I hate it here, Jake. They are all fucking crazy." She squeaks. I fall back onto the sofa and run a hand through my hair.

"It's just temporary, Willow. Make the most of the therapy classes, you'll be out…"

"Before I know it, yes, I know. Everybody keeps telling me." She snaps.

"You've got this, Willow. Anyways, how are you feeling?" I sigh, reaching for my wine. A guilty pang ripples through my heart. My sister is locked away whilst I'm cosying up to the neighbour, inviting her into her room within one day.

"I'm okay, mental health wise." She whispers, "They've drugged me up so much, all my delusions are like glued to the walls?"

"Glued to the walls?" I breathe out nervously. I never did understand the logic of delusions. When we were little, she tried to explain them to me. I didn't get it. And still don't.

"Yes. And mum seems sad?" She explains. This hurts my heart. It is even worse to hear her talk about family members. It is a painful reminder that I will never see them again, but she sees them every night. Fine, it's not in a good circumstance, but in her mind, they live on. For me, they're gone for good.

"Jake?" She whispers harshly.

"Huh? Yes, sorry, I'm here." I say quickly, "And how are the patients there?"

"There have been five fights today. Everyone likes to bark, and people are starving themselves." She replies. My lips pull together. I knew it would be a crazy house, it is the main reason I didn't want her going there. She didn't need to develop any more fears and phobias which would then turn into delusions.

"Anyways, I don't want to talk about that. I need a favour." She asks. I burrow my eyebrows together even though she can't see my face.

"What favour?"

"I need you to go down my phone, Jake." She whispers, "Find the text messages and call log. I have spoken to Mr Anderson, Olivia and Dylan on there."

My heart flutters in my chest. I shake my head.

"No, Willow, I can't. You need to stop lying to yourself..." I begin but she frantically cuts me off.

"Please, Jake!" She hisses, "Just check. I promise I'll drop it after that if they're not there."

I sigh as a lump in my throat forms.

"Fuck, I've got to go now. Someone else wants to use the phone. I will speak to you later yeah?" She tells me quickly, "Just do it, Jake. I promise I'm not crazy. You'll see."

"Speak to you later, Willow." I respond shakily. Suddenly, a long beep echoes through the phone. I rise to my feet and head towards her room. On her bed, a bag with her phone, keys and coins. The police gave it to me when I picked her up from the bar after her fight. Shakily, I unzip the bag and pull her phone out.

I open the lid. She doesn't have a code, so it unlocks quickly. Holding my breath, I click onto the phone emoji and scroll through. My heart drops in my chest. It only needs a half scroll and then I've seen every number. I feel sick as I click off and onto the messages. This is the real kicker.

"Willow." I whisper, a tear slipping down my face. My fingers tremble as I clutch onto her phone. In the messages, she has typed in random numbers. In each chat log, there are random letters. Nothing forms sentences of any type.

I scroll down. I definitely heard a ping go off that day she got the phone, so there must be at least one real person. My eyes jump to the only message with eligible sentences.

It's from O2, the phone company. My stomach lurches in my chest and my vision becomes hazy with tears.

What little hope I had for my sister is gone. It is true what they are all saying. My sister has finally lost it.

# CHAPTER TWENTY-TWO

**Willow's Pov:**

I sit in my new therapy chair, in a new therapy building. My nails curl into my skin and I scratch the rash which the dress has given me. The only positive about this location is that I am right next to a window.

I peer out at the huge wall surrounding this place. At the top of them, barbed wire curls around and around. My eyes float down to the field where a huge group of people sit. Like me, they wear the blue awful dress. One woman throws her head back as she laughs. She falls back into another woman's lap and makes no effort to move. A nurse supervising them snaps something at her, making her face contort. Slowly, the lady sits up and shuffles away. She rolls her eyes and says something, but I can't make it out. Then, she turns to face the building. I instantly recognise her as Miss Rover. Being on the bottom floor, she can stare straight into this room. Her lips twitch into a smile but it isn't warm. It's oddly terrifying and twisted.

"And how does that make you feel?" Doctor Jane pulls me back into reality.

"Huh?" I frown.

She adjusts herself in her seat with a sad look, "How does it make you feel, knowing that your brother hasn't called?"

My lips curve downwards, and I shrug. There isn't much I can say. He will not answer my calls, nor has he attempted to call me this week. A part of me knows he needs space. The other part hates him for abandoning me for a second time. It's one thing to get of me physically but to get rid of me emotionally too. That hurts.

"It is what it is." I release a sigh and look out the window again. The group has dispersed. I rub my eyes and look around, searching for them. Nothing. Not even a blade of grass out of place. Anxiously, I sit back in my seat.

"Let's talk about your delusions, shall we?" Doctor Jane smiles tightly as she peers down at her folder. My jaw hardens. I'd rather we didn't, but I don't think I have a choice.

"So, you imagined you had… what shall we call them? Friends?" She raises a quizzical eyebrow. I feel sick. Mr Anderson was more than a friend.

"They were real." I tell her sternly. *It isn't possible to do sexual acts with a delusion,* I want to tell her, but I don't want her to think I'm anymore crazy than she already labels me with.

"Were they?" She says in disbelief.

"Yes." I spit, leaning forward in my chair, "If they were not real, how comes they haven't visited me this week? Surely, if they are all in my head, they'd be in here with me too!"

Doctor Jane's lips pull into a straight line. She readjusts herself on the chair and slowly shakes her head,

"Willow, you are on stronger medicine, your delusions are not going to be as strong."

I scoff. That's not what the people on the grass think, nor my mother glued to my wall. Doctor Jane removes her glasses and scowls at me, "What's so funny?"

"Nothing." I answer quickly, "But if I can take these pills and be cured of my delusions, surely that means I don't have to be here anymore?"

"Not true." She scolds, "Willow, may I remind you, that you stopped taking your medicine on your own. It will now take another three months for the full effects of the drug to kick in. No wonder you've been having angry spells!"

"I'm going to be here for three months!" I shriek, leaping out of my chair. The doctor watches quietly as I pace back and forth. I feel like ripping my fucking hair out. The whole world thinks I'm crazy, thinks I'm dangerous. It's not like that. I know me, I know I wouldn't harm anyone.

"Did Jake find my phone?" I ask worriedly, "All the evidence is on there!"

Doctor Jane closes her eyes for a second. I watch as she takes a shaky breath and looks at me again. Her pen taps against her document. Slowly, she is losing her patience with me.

"Willow, you're exhibiting very worrying signs." She tells me, "You have to trust me, the professional. I am here to help you, but I can't help you if you're still in denial."

"How do I get better, doctor? How do I get out of here?" I snap as I fall back into my chair in exhaustion. I lean my head against my hand and stare at her expectantly, "Well, go on. Tell me, Doctor. How do I fix the shit in my head?"

"You've experienced things that nobody else has, Willow. It's not going to be an easy recovery, but I promise you it is possible." She starts but I cut her off, "Avoidance! Stop stalling, what do I have to do?"

Her lips pull into a thin line. Again, she takes a deep breath.

"First, we need to get you out of denial. You need to accept that you need help." She says slowly, "And then we work on whichever anxiety is causing you to create new people."

"Do you think I've created Mr Anderson and the others to protect me against my delusions about my parents?" I whisper quietly. It's a thought which has been playing on my mind all night. *What if everybody is correct?* It took me four years to realise Mr Fluffy was actually a delusion. *Maybe this is something similar?*

"Good, now you're getting it." Doctor Jane beams proudly at me. It feels like a part of me has died. Slowly, I'm selling myself out. 1984 is more relevant now than it ever was in class.

My doctor continues to talk about a therapy treatment plan, but I zone out. I have no choice but to follow along, so there's not much point in having a say in the matter. I look back out to the garden. My breath catches in my throat.

Amongst the tree line, Mr Anderson stands. He wears his usual smart, black suit. He is too far away to read his facial expressions, but I can feel him. He's confused. Lost. Something in me jumps for joy, he is real! He is real! My head snaps towards my Doctor.

"Doctor, look!" I exclaim. She stumbles to a pause in her conversation and follows my pointed finger.

"I told you he was real!" I cry out for joy, tearing my head back towards him. However, he's gone. My face falls and the sickness rises again.

"Willow." Doctor Jane says disappointedly, "I thought we just made a breakthrough."

I can't answer her. The lump in my throat throbs miserably and I desperately want the ground to swallow me whole. I scowl out the window and search for him. But it's true. He is not there. He was never there.

"Phone call for Willow Langly?" A nurse says as she pops her head around the door. I rise to my feet. Doctor Jane looks helplessly between me and the nurse. I can see she wants me to stay and continue the session. But we both know I won't concentrate if I know Jake is finally reaching back out.

"Fine." She sighs. I almost leap out of the room towards the phone Boothe.

"Jake?" I say quickly as soon as receiver is against my ear.

"Willow!" He exclaims. I can hear the relief in his voice.

"Where have you been?" I hiss, my eyes fogging up with tears already. I hear him choke on a sob on the other end of the phone, "Sorry Willow, I just needed time to adjust."

My stomach tightens.

"Okay." I say quietly.

"But I'm back now, and I promise I will call and come and see you as much as I can, okay?" He promises me.

"Sure."

"And I have good news." He tells me excitedly, "We have a new neighbour!"

I cast my eyes around the room. The other inmates walk past on their way to lunch. The nurses herd them in like cattle. I catch Nurse Amori's gaze. She is glaring at me but when she realises, I'm looking at her, she plasters a fake smile on her lips. Politely, she sends me a little wave. I don't send one back.

"And she is really sweet, you're going to love her!" My brother's voice rings through me. I snap back into focus.

"That's great." I say, chewing my lower lip.

"And I got a new job!" He starts rambling on again about his life. I can't help but zone out. Miss Rover walks past. My eyes are fixed on her. At this distance, I spot the awful, jagged scar down her face. The skin pulls in at her cheek and the scar wiggles up just above her eyebrow. She chats to Cow and Carly. Her face is inscrutable as they walk past me and disappear down the corridor.

"Cool." I tell my brother when I realise that he's stopped talking,

"So when will you come visit?"

"I'm not sure yet, Willow." He says, "I'm waiting for my work timetable to come through and then I will let you know as soon as possible. Okay?"

"Okay." I whisper. I take a deep breath.

"Oh, and Jake?" I mutter, "I'm starting to understand that those people might actually be all in my head."

"That's great!" He sighs in relief, "I knew you would come around to it. That makes me so happy, Willow. With this kind of progress, you will be back here in no time!"

On the other side of the room, Nurse Amori taps her watch, signalling it is time to go.

"It's lunchtime." I tell my brother wearily.

"Oh." He says, "That's okay. You get on with it, I will call you tomorrow. Same time?"

"Sure." I say before ending the call. Something bitter twists in my stomach. I haven't spoken to my brother in over a week after he abandoned me, and when he calls me again, it is about his happy life. He sounded so much lighter without me being there. The jealousy and bitterness fill me.

"Boo!" A voice calls from behind me. I jump and raise my fists in fear.

"Relax, Sugar." Miss Rover grins at me, she pushes my hands down.

"Hands!" Nurse Amori calls out bitterly, "Come on, girls, you know the no contact rule! Besides, It's lunch now. Let's go."

I scramble further away from Miss Rover; she oozes bad news. Her eye twitches when the nurse speaks.

"Where do you think we're going?" She spits rudely. Nurse Amori's jaw clenches. The two look at each other with a burning hatred. *There is definitely a story there,* I think nervously.

"Here." Miss Rover says, passing me a cigarette, "You don't want lunch. Cow didn't wash her hands."

My face contorts. I take the cigarette in my fingers.

"We are going to sit outside for lunch." Miss Rover calls out to the nurse. She doesn't even wait for her to respond before she grabs me and yanks me towards the garden area. Barely anyone sits out here. I frown as we stumble out to the broken patio underneath a green gazebo. A tall gate fences us in so we cannot get onto the large field.

"I'm Lola." Miss Rover says before popping the cigarette between her lips. I wait for her to light it, but she doesn't. Instead, she just inhales the unlit thing.

"We're not trusted with fire. For obvious reasons." She rolls her eyes before sliding down the wall to the floor. I sit next to her and bring my legs to my chest. I copy her with the cigarette.

"So, Willow, why you in here?" She frowns, pulling the cigarette from her lips to pretend to exhale. A frown coats my face, "How do you know my name?"

"Read your file." She says proudly. Mortified, I twist to face her, "How did you find my file?"

Lola shrugs but that evil, glistening look doesn't stop in her expression. She leans forward and stares into the large canteen windows. All the inmates file up in the lunch queue. Around the edges, nervous looking nurses try to contain the excited chatter.

"Keep an eye on that Nurse Amori." Lola whispers. She eyes up the security camera above our heads and leans in closer to me, "I wouldn't trust her."

"What? Why?" I stutter. She is the only nurse whose interacted with me since I got here. Apart from a couple odd looks, she hadn't given me any other reason to be sceptical.

"Just trust me." Lola hisses, "We crazies got to look out for each other in here. Let's just say when your file came into the office, she made a beeline for it."

"Why? How do you even know this?" I scowl.

Lola shrugs and takes another puff of her cigarette. I glare into the canteen windows and surely enough, Nurse Amori is watching us. Her lips are pulled into a thin line and her hands are fisted at her side. I look back to Lola cautiously.

Who can I trust? Neither woman is particularly trustworthy, and I don't want to get in between whichever feud they have going on.

"So, what are you in here for?" Lola repeats her original question. I frown at her, "You've read my file. Surely you know?"

She shakes her head and waits patiently for my answer.

"Anxiety and depression." I tell her, "With psychosis."

"Duh! Well, I know that. I mean how did you get caught?" She tries again. I blush in humiliation, "I attacked someone."

"And?" She raises an eyebrow, "It can't just be for that. Sane people beat each other up all the time."

"And I've been accused of arson." I whisper anxiously. My bottom lip rests between my lips. Her eyes widen and she smirks.

"Arson?" She scoffs, "We got another attempted murderer in here then, eh?"

My face falls.

"Unless it wasn't attempted… You succeeded, didn't you?" She blows out a breath. I freeze and look away guiltily. I could try and protest the truth, tell her that it was an accidental fire. That I don't remember anything. But look where that has got me. Nobody believes someone who is crazy.

"That's more than me, then." She sighs dramatically. My blood chills, "You tried to kill someone?"

"All right, just because I didn't succeed, it doesn't mean you can be so judgy!" She smirks, thinking I'm joking. She shoves me teasingly, but I don't smile. Her face quickly falls.

"Self-defence." She explains, "How do you think I got this scar?"

I stare back at the gruesome looking wound. It looks fairly new.

"How?" I ask her quietly. She pretends to blow out more cigarette smoke, "Someone attacked me at the canteen."

"That happened here?" I squeak in shock. My head tears towards the dozens of other people. Perhaps one of them would try to hurt me too!

"It sure did." She says bitterly, "Came from nowhere. Never even spoke to the lady who attacked me."

"It was unprovoked?" I raise an eyebrow. Lola grimaces, "Yes, but nobody believes me."

She looks at my cigarette.

"Are you going to smoke that?" She frowns. Awkwardly, I shake my head and hand it over to her. She wastes no time trying to smoke the unlit cigarette, and I'm left wondering why she didn't answer the question. She fought someone whilst in here, but that doesn't explain why she came here in the first place. Noisily, she sucks on the cigarette and coughs when the tobacco slips into her mouth.

Everything in me stills. In the distance, more people are barking, and I hear another fight break out. My fingers curl into fists and I shuffle away from Lola discreetly. She continues sucking her cigarette, whilst I try to figure out where the fuck I went wrong in my life to be grouped with these psychos.

# CHAPTER TWENTY-THREE

## Willow's Pov:

I dip my thumb in the red paint. It's cold and makes me wince but it quickly warms up against my hot skin. Careful not to drip the paint everywhere, I move my hand to the canvas. There, I delicately trace out a nose. *His* nose. Then I dip my first finger in the blue paint before creating eyebrows. *His* eyebrows.

"That's it, everybody." The art teacher beams proudly at the class, "We are working *so* well today!"

Beside me, Lola scoffs. She chews on her paint brush and scowls at the canvas. For the first time in these group therapy classes, she looks focused. Nothing could bring her out of the zone. I turn back to my painting and continue the face.

Mr Anderson stares back at me. I've created him in a multitude of different shades and colours. If he isn't real and is all in my head, why can't I make his eyes red? Or his beard yellow? He is in my imagination. He is everything I want to make him. Except real. Yes, I can't make him real.

"What are you drawing?" Lola asks. She wheels her chair behind me and peers over my shoulder. Her face contorts and she cocks her head to the side.

"My teacher." I tell her quietly. A huge smirk spreads over those plump lips.

"That's fucked up." She smiles. Despite her crude words, Lola means no harm. These last couple of days with her have been the best since arriving in this place. She is so blunt, but it adds to her appeal. You never have to worry about her thinking you're insane. Because she tells you straight up. In a way, she is a real version of Olivia. It's refreshing.

"Want to see mine?" She grins, twirling back to her own easel. She twists it around to me. It is the most beautiful water painting I've ever seen. Sure, the brush marks are all wrong and some shadows are too dark, but it makes the piece even better.

"Where is it?" I sigh, admiring the glistening lake under the darkening sky. A lone swan paddles across it, without a care in the world. Lola smiles, "A place I dream of."

Sadly, I compare our paintings. We both paint of our dreams. Only her dream could be somewhere in the world. Mine is in my head.

"Do ya wanna see mine and all?" Cow calls over to us. Both our heads snap towards the large lady jumping up and down. She throws her hands around excitedly as the dark blush coats her cheeks. Then she grabs her easel and throws it around for us to see it. Cow has painted a pair of breasts.

I blush in humiliation and avert my gaze, but Lola is furious.

"That isn't on, Cow!" She half shrieks, "That isn't on!"

Suddenly, she jumps to her feet. She throws her hand menacingly towards the lady who squeals in fear now. The laugh she had anticipated doesn't come. If I've learnt one thing about my new friend, is that she takes art class very seriously. She told me it is the one class where we are free to do what we want without judgment. I cast my eyes away from the drama about to unfold. Lola is great to me, but to the other women, she can be short tempered and volatile. I want nothing to do with it.

As usual, I'm drawn towards the green field outside the window. However, this time, there isn't just a large field with a dotted tree line. Instead, Mr Anderson is there again. I force my eyes shut and count down from ten. *He isn't real. He isn't real.* Anxiously, I reopen my eyes. But he still stands there. I tear my gaze around to the rest of the class, but nobody is looking my way. *How will I check? How will I know that he is real?*

Quietly, I get up from my seat and back up towards the window. The nurses are all preoccupied with a hysterical Lola and a sobbing Cow. I take my chance. I slip out of the door and make a beeline for the garden door. Before anybody can stop me, I sprint down the field. I feel the wind whip at my skin as I sprint faster and faster. When he sees me, a huge smile pulls onto his face.

"Mr Anderson!" I cry out in disbelief, "Liam! Liam!"

Yes, he's real! He's here! I throw myself into his arms and he swings me around in excitement. We stumble further back into the tree line.

"You're here!" I whisper into his embrace. He holds me tightly like there is no tomorrow.

"Yes, Willow. I'm here, my love." He grunts into my hair. The sound of his voice almost makes my heart explode. Timidly, I pull back suddenly.

"Are you real?" I glare up at him, grabbing his cheek. He frowns down at me, "Of course, I am real, Willow. What are you on about?"

"And Olivia? Dylan?" I panic. He nods frantically. Then, I reach back and swipe him around the face. It hurts me to hurt him, but I needed to let it out of my system.

"You, asshole!" I shriek, now the relief has passed, "Where have you been? Why have you been avoiding me?"

His face pulls into many different expressions. He struggles to keep up with my emotions. Then, I grab his hand.

"Come on, I must go show everybody that you are real!" I squeak, tugging on his arm. He freezes on the spot. I turn and yank harder, but he still doesn't relent. Nervously, he chews on his lower lip and looks behind me into the distance.

"I can't." He tells me softly. My heart drops. I scan the area but nobody else is around us. I take another deep breath and force myself to shut and open my eyes. Mr Anderson remains in front of me.

"I am real, Willow." He repeats himself, "But I can't reveal myself just yet."

"What the fuck are you on about?"

In my stomach, unease is starting to flood. Nausea makes my palms start to sweat as I stare at the beautiful man in front of me.

"My name isn't Mr. Anderson..." He starts but I cut him off, "Well, duh. You obviously have a first name. It's Liam."

"No, Willow. Well, yes. Just listen to me." He grabs me by the arm firmly before pulling out his phone. He thrusts a picture of a blonde woman in front of my face.

"Do you recognise this lady?" His eyes search mine for an answer. I frown, not understanding. I take in her pale skin and pale hair. Slowly, it clicks.

"Yes, I've seen her at the doctor's office. She is pregnant." I tell him in confusion, "What does she have to do with anything?"

"Fuck!" He growls, fisting his phone. For the first time, I see him look genuinely furious.

"What's going on?" I frown.

"That is my wife. Ex-wife. She isn't pregnant. She's played you."

"Played me? I have never met her?" I tell him, "You're frightening me. Come on, please, let me show them that you exist. That I'm not insane."

He resists again and takes a step backwards.

"Willow, this lady has been drugging you." He tells me firmly. My face scrunches up and my thoughts race one hundred miles an hour.

"That is impossible." I tell him, "I've only seen her once."

"No." He shakes his head quickly, "You've met her many times you just don't know it. I've learnt recently that she drugged me for our entire marriage. It explains so much. And then I was thinking about you and your delusions…"

He trails off into silence, not answering my burning questions. I can't move nor can I speak. I am completely broken. Everything I thought I knew had been destroyed, put back together and then destroyed again. There is so many times a crazy person can break until they actually snap for good.

"No, Liam. I've had delusions since I was ten." I hiss, "Why are you telling me all this? Why are you doing this to me?"

A solitary tear slips down my face. I don't know what is worse: believing he is imaginary or him trying to confuse me more.

"Yes, I know. But think about it, Willow. You've spiralled out of control lately. Why?" He sighs. I shake my head in disbelief, "Liam, I've been spiralling for a long time."

His lips pull together tightly.

"Did you lie to the university? Tell them I've never showed up? What about Dylan? How did you get him to say I never met him?" I whisper, the lump forming in my throat again. It hurts too much to not ask the question, but I know the answer is going to hurt more.

"Yes." He confesses before growing frantic in his movements, "but that's only because I realised my wife, Emily, has been stalking you. You're safer here than out there, Willow. And Dylan didn't take much convincing to lie."

He turns his nose up in a scoff with that last comment. The rage floods through me.

"What!" I shriek, "You threatened him? And you let everybody think I am crazy just to keep me from your crazy ex?"

"To keep you safe." He protests.

"No!" I bark, "You don't get to make that decision for me. People don't get to make that decision for me!"

"Willow..." He trails off into silence and tries to pull me close. I yank my arm away and stumble backwards. My vision fogs up more and more with tears.

"If she is drugging people, why don't you go to the police? Why take my freedom away?" I choke on a sob. Liam's face hardens and I watch as he strains. There is something he isn't telling me.

Suddenly, a voice of a nurse calls out my name. She shouts over and over again. I peer out of the treeline and see a little blue hat on the horizon.

"Meet me here in three days." He tells me frantically.

"No, don't go yet!" I squeak. I can't bear to go back to being in the crazy house, surrounded by real nut cases. I am here by accident. I need him to help me escape. He has proven that I am not insane!

"Meet me here in three days, Willow. Tell me you will." He says, searching my eyes for an answer. I wince at his cold tone.

"I-I promise." I tell him shakily.

"Good." He says before slamming his lips against my own. It melts me in more ways than one. It a kiss of a lifetime. A real, true kiss. I feel drunk as my mind swarms with so many questions. Suddenly, he pulls back. Without looking back, he disappears out of view. My whole-body trembles in fear.

I stumble up the hill towards the nurse. She scowls at me as she grabs me violently by the arm.

"Where have you been?" She hisses, "You know you're not allowed outside without supervision!"

"I'm sorry, Miss." I give her an award-winning smile, "I just wanted some fresh air."

She doesn't soften at all. If anything, her grip becomes worse and worse on my arm. Her nails prick me, making me yelp.

"Ow, nurse Amori!" I gasp, pulling away. She doesn't relent as she drags me back inside.

Suddenly, the world around me becomes a rush and a blur. The walls seem to bleed and the world drips into a blurred mess. I stumble around and grab at anything to keep me steady. However, I'm falling to the floor before I can stop myself. I feel my whole body smack the cold ground with a thud and the pain quickly follows. My lips won't even move to scream or cry. The only thing I can move are my eyes. They flick to Lola in the corner of the corridor. She watches with wide eyes. A look of pure terror flickers on her face.

And then everything goes dark.

# CHAPTER TWENTY-FOUR

**Jake's Pov:**

"No, Jake you have to believe me." She begs down the phone. My heart throbs in my chest and I feel sick. She had made so much progress, only to relapse again. Doctor Jane said these things might happen. It doesn't stop the pain when it does happen though.

"They checked CCTV; you were with nobody." I sigh. I can hear her get frustrated on the other end.

"That is because we were in the bushes!" She shrieks. I raise my eyebrows even though she can't see me. I flip the pancake over in the pan before pouring out the hot water into two mugs. The sweet smell of sugary pancakes and tea fills my nose.

"Jake, why are you fighting with me on this? I am your sister!" Her voice breaks as she talks. I push back the threatening tears as I tuck the phone between my shoulder and ear, so I have free hands to pour the milk into the tea. I stir it and bring it into Alice who is fast asleep in Willow's bed still. Carefully, I place it on the side before quickly returning to the pancakes.

"Because you are insane, Willow." I snap at her. My entire life, I have been nothing but understanding. Beating up the taunting bullies, standing up to our parents and anyone who looks down on her for being not all there. All I'm asking of her is to get the help she needs.

"That's real nice, Jake. Thanks." She responds bitterly.

"Well, what do you want me to say?" I hiss plating up the pancakes, "That the man you've conjured up in your head surprisingly showed up to the hospital, nobody saw him, there is no camera footage, nothing! He's accusing a woman we've never met of drugging you and him. It's too much, Willow! It's too crazy! Am I supposed to take a leap of faith?"

"What do you have to lose?" She spits.

"You!" I half shriek before quickly lowering my voice so I don't wake Alice up, "I have you to lose, Willow! If you keep insisting that these people are real, you will be locked away forever. What part of that do you not understand?"

"So, you want me to ignore the truth?"

"Fucksake, Willow. You're not listening." I snap, "Stop acting like a stroppy child. These people are in your head. Mum, Dad, Mr Anderson. The lot of them!"

A long silence drifts between us.

"I've got to go." She whispers before hanging up the phone. My jaw drops in disbelief. You can't coddle her and let her believe these fantasies. But at the same time, if you don't, you push her further into the world of make belief. It's an impossible gamble.

Furiously, I throw my phone across the room. She is impossible to deal with. I slouch over the kitchen counter and hang my head.

"Are you okay?" Alice calls from behind me. I startle and spin around to her. Quickly, I plaster a fake smile to my lips.

"Of course." I say, "I made breakfast!"

She clings to the cup of tea I made her whilst staring at the pancakes on the side. She licks her lips, "They smell great."

I beam at her before passing her a plate of food. We collapse onto the sofa and tuck into the sugary goodness.

"So, who were you on the phone to? It sounded heated." She says sadly before popping some food in her mouth. I feel grim even thinking about the argument.

"Wait, you don't have to tell me, sorry!" She squeaks, "It's not my place."

My heart flutters at her kindness. She genuinely just wants to make me feel better. This past week, she has been nothing but caring and gentle. We spent nearly every waking moment together when we are not at work. I place a hand on her knee and smile at her.

"It's fine." I whisper, "It was my sister."

"What's wrong with her?"

I scoff at her poor choice of words. She winces as if she's said something wrong. I let the silence sift between us before I sigh. The beautiful woman in front of me scowls.

"I haven't exactly been truthful to you about my sister." I mutter, turning to face her, "My sister isn't on holiday. She's actually in a mental hospital."

"Oh!" Alice squeaks, covering her mouth in shock, "poor thing! Which one?"

"The one down the road from here actually. So, she's close enough, but yeah. She needs help."

"And how are you doing?" She shuffles closer towards me, "It must be difficult for you too. To lose your sister like that. The guilt or anger with the situation. It must be *so* hard."

"Yeah." I frown.

"Sorry." She smiles sadly, "I used to be a social worker before my boyfriend came along. I'd help children, particularly with special educational needs. Their families were always greatly affected if the child had to go into care or into more specialised hospitals."

My heart constricts even more. She is perfect. She understands everything, if not more.

"It's been hard." I confess with a deep sigh, "She has severe delusions but won't listen to me when I say they are not real."

"What are the delusions about?" She raises an eyebrow before popping another spoonful of pancake into her mouth. I stare at the floor bitterly. I know I can trust Alice, but it's never easy confessing Willow's delusions. They are too odd. It's easy to judge.

"A bit of everything really. Usually, she has delusions about people or animals. So, like our parents. She still sees them every day since their death." I whisper. Alice places our plates on the counter before wrapping an arm around me. My head falls onto her shoulder and her sweet perfume fills my senses. It's intoxicating.

"I understand. One of my students used to hallucinate about their dead dog. Though, apparently the dog could tap dance and sing." She lets out a little laugh. It lightens the mood and I'm thankful for it.

"Delusions are weird." I agree, "I mean, this new one she has, is difficult. She has thought up a professor and the class. Every day, she was going elsewhere but believing she was at university, studying for her exams."

"How strange." She whispers, "Does she still see them?"

"No, well, yes. She saw the professor yesterday apparently. But she hasn't seen any of the others." I scowl before pulling back to run a hand through my hair. Alice's face is pale, but she smiles quickly. For a second, I think I have frightened her off. It's never easy having to hear about somebody's delusions. Deep down, every living person is afraid of the *what if*. What if there is somebody invisible standing over you right now? What if the strange being wants to hurt you? Our only consolation is the fact we cannot interact with this other realm. Unfortunately for Willow, she can. Realm or imagination, it doesn't matter. The fact she is interacting with frightening things that nobody else can see must be extremely difficult.

"Thank you for sharing that with me." She says quietly. I look into her eyes and for a second, all my troubles disappear. Her small fingers fumble with mine, and the touch is electrifying. Slowly, I lean towards her. She quickly closes the gap and kisses me. My body almost explodes from the contact. Her fingers lace into my hair as she deepens the kiss. I groan. She tastes *so* good.

Her hand jumps down to the zip on my trousers but I pull away.

"Just relax." She breathes against my lips, "let me help you."

I blink rapidly in disbelief. She doesn't give me another moment to think about it. Instantly, she sits on my lap and kisses me again. My head lulls back as her fingers scratch up and down my chest. It feels like everything becomes hazy as she removes my trousers. My heartbeat quickens and my mouth becomes dry.

"That's it." She whispers seductively before hoisting her skirt up. I blink back the confusion and continue to kiss her. But it's too difficult to stay in the present, I feel exhausted.

"Wait." I moan, pushing her back slightly. She kisses down my neck which hushes my protests. I groan in approval and let her continue. She's right. I need to relax. I need to take a step away from being the older, protective brother, and instead enjoy the young adult life.

# CHAPTER TWENTY-FIVE

**Willow's Pov:**

"Yeah, and then she came up to me and slapped me around the face because I took her phone call slot." Lola moans, rubbing a red patch on her face. She got into a fight earlier, and she has repeated the story over twenty times. It's as if she cannot regulate her emotions and ranting is the only way forward.

"It literally came out of nowhere, that stupid bitch." She snorts and her head tips back, "I sure showed her. I bet the nurses are going to come get me any minute, you know? I fucked her up pretty badly."

Not really listening, I check my watch before casting my gaze around the canteen. It is pretty full, and the nurses race around, trying to contain the madness. My bottom lip bleeds from how much I nibble on it. The anxiety creeps higher and higher in my chest. I check my watch again.

"Okay, what is it?" Lola crinkles her nose. Her gaze sinks into my face and she looks at me in frustration. "If you check your watch one more time, I think I am going to break it. Are you even listening to me?"

"Hmm? What?" I say half-heartedly, stealing another glance at my watch. In five minutes, I am meeting Mr Anderson again. The long hand on the clock ticks. Four minutes.

"Ah, shit." Lola sighs, and I follow her gaze to see four nurses wearing protective gear storming into the room.

*Shit.* My heart drops in my chest. My plan had been to sneak off, but Lola has drawn attention to us. How am I going to escape outside when there are a half a dozen more nurses in the room.

"Make a scene." I hiss to Lola, never taking my eyes off the nurses who scan the room, searching for her.

"What?" She gawps in shock.

I turn and grab her by the arm, "I will explain later. Kick off. Start another fight. I need to go somewhere."

Flushed cheeks, she watches me intently, but then a smirk rests on her cheeks. "I thought you would never ask. I've been looking for an excuse to fight those cunts."

She sends me a wink before jumping to her feet. Shocked, I watch as she meets the nurses across the room, fist held up in the air. A war cry leaves her lips as she throws her limbs around, meeting the nurses' body. Grunts and cries of shock fill the room. With the distraction, I take my chance to escape.

Head low, I keep my body pressed against the wall as I stalk around the room, before slipping out of sight. The nurses which usually guard the door are now prying Lola's screaming body off a guard who cries in pain as she sinks her nails into his cheek.

The winter air slashes at my face as I sprint down the hill like my life depends on it. My heart threatens to jump out of my chest and my lungs heave. I eventually stumble down to the meeting spot, and there he is.

Hunched over, Mr Anderson sits on the muddy ground, chewing nervously at his fingernails. Upon hearing me, he shoots to his feet. Before I know it, he has his arms wrapped around my waist and his lips are pressed firmly against mine. I soak in the delicious taste of whisky and cigarettes as my fingers play with his beard which has now grown out.

"Willow." He moans against my lips, making my heart flip in my chest.

I respond quickly, "Liam."

"I've missed you so much." He tells me, and his voice cracks slightly. I shake my head against his lips, "I promise you that I've missed you more. Thank God you're real. You don't understand how hard it has been."

My fingers jump to the buttons on his shirt and I quickly pull them apart so that I can touch his warm chest. He bristles under my touch, and a low groan leaves his lips.

"I don't have long before they notice I'm missing." I whisper quickly before working on his jeans. He hesitates. "Willow, are you sure?"

"Prove to me how real you are." I grin, pulling him back against my lips. This seems to make him snap. His hand shoots to his jeans and he quickly frees himself from his pants. My jaw drops as I see how hard he is already for me. Slowly, I wrap my fingers around his cock and I thrust, and at the same time, his hand cups my mound under my dress.

"You're soaked." He groans in approval, and I think my legs might give way when his thumb touches my clit. A strained noise leaves his lips as he pulls away and uses his other hand. I stop and grab the first hand, pulling the scarred thumb to my lips.

"Don't." His voice is strained.

"What happened to it?" I press a light kiss to the tip.

"Emily. Emily happened."

My eyes go round, "She stabbed you?"

"She sliced it open with a glass bottle. I tried to leave her, and she decided to assault me." He whispers, pulling away from me, but I don't let him get far. I yank his thumb back to my lips and press more kisses up and down it. He watches in shock as I let it slip past my lips.

"Fuck, Willow." He groans as my other continues to pump his cock.

"Let me replace the memory." I say in a sultry voice before licking up his thumb. I suck it like it's his cock and he groans in approval, head falling back. I let my teeth gently scrape it, earning another beautiful noise to slip from his mouth.

"I can't take it much longer." He grunts before grabbing my hips and pushing me up against the tree. I wrap my legs around him as he lines himself up. Then, with one thrust, he forces himself inside of me and I cry out in pleasure.

"Liam!" I squeal, nails digging into his arms. The pleasure builds quickly- too quickly- and I squeeze around his cock. With one hand under my ass, propping me up, he uses the other to flick my clit, earning another long mewl from me. It seems to spur him on. Faster, and harder he thrusts.

"That's it, Willow. Take it. Take my cock." He growls. Something wild flashes in his eyes, and it almost sends me over the edge.

"You will never doubt yourself again, okay? I am as real as they come. Somebody who isn't real couldn't do this to you." He thrusts hard inside of me, and the hand on my ass slips lower. One of his fingers tease my asshole and I scream in pleasure. He draws circles around it, before dipping in.

Before I can stop it, I explode around him, crying out his name into his shoulder, desperately trying to keep my voice down. He doesn't relent his thrusting.

"One down, two more to go." He grins, before pulling out and dropping to his knees. My fingers fist his hair in shock, but I don't get a moment to process what he is doing before his tongue laps greedily at my clit.

"Fuck, your cum tastes so good." He groans, and the vibrations only push me closer to the edge again. He slips a finger inside of me and continues his assault on my clit. His other hand reaches up and holds my chest. He keeps me pinned up against the tree, and I'm thankful. My legs threaten to give way.

"Liam!" I croak as I feel my release pending. His assault comes faster, more precise on the spot I desperately want. "Cum again, baby. Cover my face in your cum."

On cue, I fall over the edge with a muffled scream. I feel my tongue bleed from how hard I'm biting it. Just as I calm down, he pushes his fingers back up, and one slips inside my asshole. With lustful eyes, he watches as I explode again, though this time I can't contain my scream. My entire body shakes and trembles as I come down and he helps me ride it out.

"God, Liam." I whisper breathlessly against his lips when he stands back up. I reach for his cock, but he pulls away.

"I want to make you-" I begin but he cuts me off with a quick shake of his head.

"No. The next time I cum, I want you to be free. I will not have my release whilst you're stuck in this shit hole. It is my doing."

"It is not your fault!" I say, but then stumble over my words. It *is* his fault, surely. He lied, he deceived everyone. But then again, he did it to protect me. My brain rushes with confusion.

"It's okay, my dear." He whispers, pressing his lips against my forehead, "You'll be out soon, and then we can decide whose fault it was. In the meantime, stay strong for me."

"You're going?" I yelp, fingers clasping around his arm.

His eyes bear into mine, "I will be back tomorrow and I will tell you the whole truth. Say you'll meet me again."

"Yes, of course, I will."

"Good." He says breathlessly, before leaving me with one last kiss.

# CHAPTER TWENTY-SIX

## Willow's Pov:

He didn't show up. Mr. Anderson didn't show up for our visit. I waited an extra hour, before a nurse found me sitting at the bottom of the hill miserably and escorted me back to my room.

I shove the heavy door open and slip into my bedroom. On the far side of the room, my mother is still glued to the wall. I frown at her. Today, she has no face. And she feels totally numb. Instead of her usual haunting, today, mum is just a wax figure.

"Evening." I tell her weakly before dropping myself onto the bed. Suddenly, something scrunches. I shoot up from the bed and pull the covers back. My heart catches in my chest when I look at the piece of paper. It is a page torn out of 1984. At the top, one quote has been highlighted: *"Under the spreading chestnut tree, I sold you and you sold me: There lie they, and here lie we, under the spreading chestnut tree."*

The room starts to spin as I clutch onto the page tighter and tighter. *What does this mean? Did Mr Anderson put this here? Has he been in my room?*

I crunch the paper to make sure it is real. But even that could be a delusion.

"Fuck." I croak as a tear slips down my face. All the unanswered questions haunt me.

A knock at the door yanks me from my miserable thoughts. Before I can answer, the door begins to open. I panic and hide the page under my pillow. Nobody can find out about this. A lump in my throat forms.

Lola slips in and quickly closes the door behind her. Fright stains her face, and she wears a busted lip and bruised eye. There is a numb look flashing in her eyes; it is so different to her usual rage-filled glares.

"Are you okay?" I bounce up and grab her by the arms. She flinches at my touch and pulls away.

"I escaped inclusion." She heaves breathlessly, "It's awful in there, Willow. Fuck. It's only been twenty-four hours. There are only so many white walls someone can take before they go insane. Sometimes I think they created that place to create crazy people. Not heal them."

I remain silent and let her rant at me.

Her miserable eyes bear into mine, "Please tell me it was worth it. What did you escape for?"

A deep blush burns my face, "I saw my professor."

She raises an eyebrow, "The one you painted?"

"Yes."

"The one that isn't real?" Her nose crinkles in disgust. I shake my head quickly, and the guilt eats me up. She was being hurt and tortured whilst I had my legs wrapped around Mr Anderson's face.

"He is real." I tell her slowly.

She throws her hands to her hips angrily, "Oh yeah? Where is he? Is he in the room with us now?"

I awkwardly look at my mum who doesn't seem to flinch, and then back at Lola.

"No. He's not."

"Fuck, Willow." She exclaims in frustration before falling onto my bed.

"I'm sorry you're going through this. How much longer are you supposed to be in there? How did you even escape?" I awkwardly sit next to her and place a reassuring hand on her knee.

A scoff passes her lips, "Two weeks I'm in there for. And all it took was some stupid male nurse. I asked to go to the toilet. I think he is new. He doesn't know the toilet trick. For future reference, you can go through the ceiling in the furthest toilet. It takes you to the courtyard." She beams like it's the best thing she has ever discovered. I gulp.

"Anyway, it doesn't matter." She suddenly softens, "It's not really your fault. I beat that girl up, and I was always going to fight the nurses. You just prompted me to do it quicker than expected." She grins, and just like that, the tension simmers away, and the shaky breath returns to my lungs.

"Anyway, how is that bitch nurse Amori treating you?" She sighs, throwing her hands above her head, "I saw she sedated you the other night."

"She did?" I gawp in shock. Lola purses her lips, and glares angrily up at the ceiling.

"Lola? What do you mean?"

"She drugs everyone, you're not special." She suddenly bites back, "It's like a power trip to her. When she can't be bothered to defuse a situation, she will stab you unknowingly to knock you out. Nurses are allowed to sedate you in extreme cases. But for her, it's like an hourly occurrence. The side effects are fucking awful."

"That must be illegal!" I shoot up in shock, "When my brother finds out about this…" I hiss under my breath. Lola lets out a vicious laugh.

"What's he going to do about it, huh? Call the police? Shout from the roof tops that you, a delusional inmate with violent tendencies, feels she was drugged by the caring nurse sent here to look after everybody?" Lola spits. Her eyes are cold and hard as they jump around my face. I visibly flinch at her bluntness. Slowly, I shake my head. I want to say something, to protest but the words in my mouth are mush.

"See?" Lola hisses, "We have no power here. Nobody believes a crazy person, other than another crazy person."

"It's not fair." I scream, throwing myself to the floor. I fist my fingers in my hair and sob. My anger turns to blame; I want to accuse everybody of ruining my life. My brother, my doctor, *Mr Anderson.* They're slowly suffocating me by being controlling.

"Checks." A nurse says as she pops her head around the door. Nurse Amori stares in at us. My jaw hardens as I watch the awful lady's gaze flicker between us two.

"You shouldn't be in here, Lola." She hisses, "It's against protocol. Wait. Aren't you supposed to be in inclusion?"

"You know what else is against protocol?" Lola snaps, "Drugging inmates."

I wince in shock at her bravery. Nurse Amori's lips twitch upwards in a twisted smile, "What are you on about now, Lola?"

"You." She protests, jumping to her feet, "You won't get away with this!"

A long silence drifts between us three. Warily, I watch Nurse Amori and Lola have a face off. I doubt myself. Nurse Amori couldn't have drugged us. CCTV would have caught her, or at least another nurse. *It's just not possible!* But then I did black out. *Was this just another episode or...*

"Won't I?" She smirks, cocking her head to the side. My gaze snatches up at her.

"You bitch!" Lola shrieks. Nurse Amori stumbles backwards and pulls on her walkie talky. She gives us both a malicious smile before clicking the green button.

"I'm requesting back up!" She pants, feigning fear, "Miss Rover and Miss Langly have threatened me."

I shoot to my feet and shake my head quickly.

"That's not true!" I protest but Nurse Amori quickly takes her finger off the recording button. My heart sinks as a chorus of stomping echoes around in the hallway.

"Fuck this!" Lola shrieks before pouncing onto Nurse Amori. The two women violently throw punches at each other, and rip at each other's hair. I stumble forward to join in but I'm instantly frozen to the floor. Lola rips at Nurse Amori's hair, and it slips backward. Blonde tendrils of hair flash into view.

Nausea rises in my chest.

Nurse Amori strikes Lola around the face. Her sharp nails slice through her cheek. Blood tumbles from the wound. Before I can do anything, I stumble to the floor. It feels as though I'm tumbling through different dimensions at the sight of the blood. My throat closes up and the tears sting my eyes. Everything shakes and I struggle to catch a breath. My knees hiss in pain from where I land funny. Frantically, my fingers tug at my hair.

The delusions harass me. *The Fire. My family. Mr Anderson.* I see them all bleeding, pouring from every hole in their body. Their miserable shrieks echo around my head.

"No!" I cry out, "No! No! No!"

It doesn't help. The images and sounds increase double fold.

I shake and struggle for breath. Suddenly, a mass of nurses burst into the room. I watch as they rip Lola from them. She fights back with every inch of strength. A louder chorus of groans and whimpers fill the room as she pummels everybody. It makes my suffering so much worse. A nurse beside the fight fills up a sedative drug into a needle. She thrusts it towards Nurse Amori who quickly stabs Lola in the thigh. Her violent protests suddenly weaken. Spasms take a hold of Lola. She twitches and jolts, her mouth opening and closing in protest. No noise comes out. Finally, her eyes flutter close, and her entire body turns limp.

Mortified, I watch as Nurse Amori turns towards me. She has fixed her wig again. My fingers clench into fists but I don't get the luxury of a fight. Suddenly, the nurses grab each of my limbs and pull me out so I'm like a starfish. Nurse Amori advances towards me with a new needle. I scream out but the words are snatched from my panicking mind.

She brings her lips close to my ear so that nobody else can hear.

"This is going to hurt a lot." She grins before inserting the needle. I cry out in pain; it feels as though my arm is on fire as the liquid spreads through my veins. My whole-body tenses up.

"Take her to ward four, please." Nurse Amori switches to become more professional. The nurses drag me across the corridor. I beg my body to move but I am completely frozen, the only thing that moves are my eyes. I squeeze them shut as the light around me grows brighter and brighter. I only open them again when I feel myself get thrown into a bed.

A commotion of noise echoes around me as each of the nurses connect me up to different monitors. Despite not being able to move my body, I can feel everything. The slapping on my veins, the pinching of my skin followed by the sting of the needle. In my mind, I scream out.

"Check her vitals." Nurse Amori instructs as she barges into the room. I lose myself in the medical chatter. The monitor behind me beeps in tune to my heartbeat.

"That will be all." She says to the people surrounding me, all dressed in blue and white. They each bow their heads before scuttering out the room. Finally, I hear the last person leave. I feel the fear increase inside of me at the realisation I am completely defenceless, in a room alone with the malicious head nurse.

"Oh, Willow." She tuts, crossing the room. I hear the slapping of plastic as she pulls the gloves up her arms, "Figure out who I am yet?"

That malicious grin grows and grows until I fear it might fall of the side of her face. My eyes are wide and fearful.

"Oh, come on. Blonde hair? Jealous lover?" She rolls her eyes, "Fine, my name begins with an E."

*Emily.*

The world around me becomes a humming mess.

"You just had to be difficult, didn't you?" She scolds, returning to my bedside. Violently, she grabs my cheeks and tosses my head side to side.

"I really did want to keep you alive; you know. I thought discrediting you enough to get you locked up would be good enough. But no. You didn't make it easy for me." She hisses, "But drawing pictures of him? Secretly meeting him in the garden? Starting rumours that I drug people?"

My eyes widen as she picks up a needle from the counter next to me. I beg my body to move, to make myself scream. *She is crazy!*

"Liam is mine. Got it?" She smirks, bringing her face close to me, "You just seem to keep getting in the way."

*The questions flood my mind. Why now? Liam said she left him. Why does she want him back?*

"Now, now, you pretty little thing. Don't hurt yourself by thinking too much." She strokes my cheek patronisingly and it makes me feel sick, "Remember the pale monster ten years ago? Who do you think that was?"

*Fuck.*

"That's right!" Her eyes light up happily, "I'm your daddy's little mistress. And I would have stayed that way if you would have shut up talking about the pale monster to your mummy."

My thoughts race faster and faster in my head. The fear switches to rage. *The malicious bitch!*

"And I've also met your brother." She points out with a devilish smirk, "Oh, wait no. I've *slept* with your brother."

I scream out in my head and try to drown out her words. It's not true, it can't be true! Jake couldn't have. Then, a bitter thought seeps into my head. He spoke about a new neighbour; about a woman he likes. I feel the tears burn in my eyes. *Why is she doing all of this? What does she gain from ruining my family's life?*

"Great question." She smirks as if she can read my mind, "Why am I doing all of this?"

She pulls out a vial from her pocket and unscrews the cap. I watch in horror as she measures out a dose.

"Nobody has ever rejected me, Willow. I mean look at me. I'm gorgeous." She hisses, "And yet your daddy decided to cut all contact one day. Nine months ago. Why? Why did he stop talking to me? Oh, that's right. You started dreaming about the pale monster again, and you got a little too specific. How many times did you see me? How many times did your daddy tell you that you were crazy?" She hums merrily to herself before flicking the needle, and some droplets fly out.

"It just so happens that he died a week later. Oh, and the malicious bitch who kept us from seeing each other. That's your mum, of course." She says viciously. It feels like someone has punched me in the stomach. If I could move, I think I'd be physically sick. *Was it her? Did she create the fire?*

In the corner of the room, something moves. I stare in fear at my mother. She burns brightly, eyes twisting back in her head until they are dark, white balls. A rage seeps through her, it makes me hurt. It's as if the fire is pumping through my own body.

"You should be thanking me," Nurse Amori growls, as she returns her vicious grasp around my face, "I could have let you die in that fire. But no, I had some mercy."

I want to scream out of her that she doesn't know the meaning of mercy. *Torturing someone with the belief they murdered their parents. That they are crazy?* That is the complete opposite of mercy!

"You had to take all the blame, of course, so that they would never look further than immediate family. Though, even if they did, they wouldn't have found me. I cover my tracks very well." She boasts. A larger lump forms in my throat as she waves the needle in front of my face.

"Now, of course, I'm only telling you all this because you're going to die very soon." She confesses, "You *and* Liam."

My heart almost lurches out of my chest. *What has she done with him? Is he safe?* That's why he didn't visit me! I knew he wouldn't give up on us!

"Don't worry about your little lover. He's bad news." She whispers, running a hand down my face. My eyes dart back to my mother who seems to melt. It's as if she's made of wax and the fire is slowly pulling her apart. Her shrieks quickly follow the visuals. My eyes squeeze shut in misery. *Why is this happening to me?*

"Long story short, I hate your family. Daddy rejected me for mummy. You are sleeping with my ex-husband, and even before that, you were becoming suspicious of your delusions and the affair. Nothing that a drug couldn't fix. And finally, your brother used me as emotional support. You know, he never stopped talking about you?"

My stomach flips in my chest. The tears tumble down my face faster and faster. The salt burns my skin.

"And now you die, alongside your lover." She whispers with a small smile, "Wherever he might be."

She sends me a malicious wink before grabbing my arm. My body cries out, but I am completely helpless. She is totally in control, just like she had planned. Then, she thrusts the needle into my arm. The cold liquid pours into my veins like liquid fire.

It's agonising. Worse than agony.

I silently pray that I die quickly.

# CHAPTER TWENTY-SEVEN

**Jake's Pov:**

"Where is it?" I frown, chucking another box to the side. Frustrated, I turn around and stare at Willow's messy room. Her stuff is everywhere and yet I can't find the book. My memory is hazy from last night and yet I distinctly remember Alice putting a book in her bag before she left for the shops. Willow's University book. I stumble over another box and fall to the floor. My knees scream in pain as I land awkwardly. Frustratedly, I run a hand through my hair and take deep breaths. Perhaps I am imagining things? What would Alice want with Willow's school textbook? And yet something deep down tells me something is wrong.

A knock at the door pulls me from my thoughts. I leap over the mess and close the door behind me before heading towards the noise. Before I even reach the door, three more knocks come out.

"Coming!" I holler before swinging the door open. A thin looking woman stares back at me. With bright red hair and a horrifying dress sense, she captures me instantly.

"Yes?" I frown, closing the door slightly. She wipes her clammy hands on her black dress.

"My name is Olivia Wright. I go to University with Willow." She says quickly, "Can I come in?"

I stumble backwards and look her up and down. My heart races faster and faster in my chest.

"You're Olivia?" I gasp. *She's real?* Willow wasn't making her up! Olivia takes another step towards me. Her eyes are red and puffy, and she looks like she hasn't slept in days.

"Yes, now can I come in? It's urgent." She hisses. I open the door and take a step back. She hurries into the house, glaring around at everything. I watch in awe as she charges around my small house, taking it all in. Eventually, she stumbles into the kitchen. Her eyes land on Alice's handbag. Suddenly, she grabs it and twists around to face me.

"Whose bag is this?" She spits. I frown and try to pull it from her fingers, "None of your business. Why are you here?"

"Jake, tell me. I fear for Willow's safety. Has a blonde lady been visiting you?" Olivia barks, throwing the bag to the floor. I shake my head once, and then twice, more confidently, "No."

Olivia's eyes scan my face for a long moment. I can see the cogs turning in her brain as she tries to figure out if I'm telling the truth or not. Finally, she yanks out her phone and thrusts a photo in front of my face. A blonde Alice stares back at me.

"Do you know this lady?" Olivia frowns. I feel my whole body start to shake in fear, "Yes, she's our new neighbour? What has she got to do with Willow?"

"Fuck!" She hisses, "I can't find Liam. He's been missing for a couple days; we were hunting Emily down trying to find her. And then Willow went missing too. And I've lost eyes on Emily."

"What? Slow down!" I panic, "Who is Liam? Who is Emily?"

Olivia watches me miserably, "Liam is Mr Anderson and Emily is his wife. Well, ex-wife. She is the woman you've been seeing.

*Alice.*"

Her whole-body slumps as she falls onto the sofa. I am speechless as I stumble towards her. She runs her fingers through her hair and a small sob escapes her lips.

"So, Willow was telling the truth? You all exist?" I whisper before growing angry, "But he denied he knew her! We couldn't find you either! And Dylan denied it too... Did you purposely hide from us? From the police?"

"No, Jake! Listen to yourself, for God's sake!" She suddenly explodes. I slam my lips shut as she shoots upwards. She shoves a feisty finger against my chest.

"You don't know Emily like I do, that bitch is bad news! She hid us from you, and when we found out, it was too late." She hisses, "It's not like Liam could have done anything. Emily is brilliant at discrediting people. Willow is just another one of her victims."

"Why?" I whisper, "Why Willow?"

Nervously, Olivia chews on her fingernails. She gives me a sad look before sighing, "Okay, I can tell you but you're going to have to believe me. It sounds crazy, it sounds unbelievable. But that is because Emily is crazy and unbelievable. I've only just put the pieces together, but it was too late. Willow and Liam are gone."

Mortified, I take a seat on the sofa. Olivia explains it all. My Dad's affair, the fire, the victim blaming, the drugs. I sit quietly and take it all in. My entire body shakes with guilt and rage. Willow had tried to warn me; she had tried to convince me she was telling the truth and I didn't believe her. I hadn't even given her another chance. And then I slept with the woman who had it out for her.

Weakly, I hang my head in shame. I feel Olivia's arm snake around my shoulders.

"Look, I know you're feeling sad or whatever, but we need to go." She tells me sternly, "In that hospital, Willow is an easy target. And now that Liam's gone, I think Emily is finishing everyone off. We know too much. I need your car. It's too far to run, and there are no taxis available!"

I shoot up from the sofa and grab my keys. Olivia leads the way as I stumble around with my phone. I call the hospital. Once and then twice. There is no answer. On the third time, I get through to someone.

"Hello, my name is Jake Langly, Willow Langly's brother. Can I speak to her?" I pant as I race towards the car. I stick the call on speaker and throw my seatbelt on. Olivia slides in next to me. The car lurches forward as I throw my foot on the accelerator.

"Willow langly, you say." The receptionist hums. I hear them type at the computer. A long silence follows. I tear the car around the corner

"Ah, yes, I was just going to call you, Jake. It seems your sister has had a particularly damaging delusion this afternoon." The receptionist says. I hiss and speed faster to the hospital.

"What do you mean?" I growl, "Where is she now? Put her on the phone!"

Olivia clings on tightly to her seat. Her face is pale and blank. This isn't good news.

"Not to worry, Sir. She's been sedated. When she is awake, we can put her on the phone." The receptionist says. I lose my cool.

"What!" I howl, "You do not have my permission to sedate her! I specifically ticked the box on the registration form to say no interference."

"I appreciate that, Sir. However, this was an emergency. And as per our insurance policy, if an inmate becomes violent towards staff, we reserve the right to act in whichever we see fit to have the safest outcome." The receptionist dutifully reads out her script. My fingers tighten on the steering wheel as we lurch around the roundabout.

"I'm on my way. I'd like to see her." I snap.

"You can't, Sir. She's in the ward. Visitors are not allowed in that part of the facility. You are more than welcome to wait in the sitting room, though."

I lurch forward and hang up the call. Olivia chokes on a sob as the tears stream down her face.

"How well do you know the hospital?" I ask her. She shakes her head, "Not at all. Liam visited her last week, but he's gone. I never got to find out..."

"You must know something!" I interrupt. Everything shakes and my own guilt makes me feel sick. Willow told the truth this entire time. And yet I treated her like everybody else. We didn't acknowledge her feelings.

I yank the car into the car park and jump out. A large blue signpost directs us towards the wards. I race towards it, with Olivia quick on my heel.

"What are you going to do, Jake?" She calls after me, "They won't let you in."

I slow down as we come to the windows. Frantically, I check every single one, desperately hoping to find her.

"I don't care, I'll hurt anyone who gets in my way. Willow will not suffer for my disbelief." I snap, racing to the next window. And then I spot her.

My weak, little sister is strapped up against the bed. Wires stick out of every part of her body, all connecting to different machines. Her eyes flutter open and close. It pulls at my heart strings to see how weak she looks.

Then, I see Alice. *Emily*. She picks up a needle from the side and removes a dial from her coat pocket. Droplets fly out the top when she flicks it. Willow's eyes become wide as she stares at it.

"Why isn't she moving? Why isn't she protesting?" I hiss towards Olivia. Frightened, Olivia throws her hand to her mouth. Another tear trickles down her face, "She's sedated. She won't be able to move."

My fingers try to yank at the window frames, but it's no use. I can't get in. I pull my hand back to bang on the window. Perhaps if we can distract Emily she will stop. Just as I go to smack it, Olivia grabs me.

"Security!" She gasps. I tear my gaze left and three guards charge towards us. I give my sister one final look before sprinting away, looking for another way in.

"This way!" Olivia hisses as she charges towards the exit sign on a door. She yanks it open, and we quickly slip into the corridor. A nurse scowls at us as we sprint past. The smell of ammonia makes me feel sick and the squeaky floors makes it hard to stay upright.

"Left!" I call out to her when we come to a crossroad in the corridors. My mind races as I try to work out which room she'd be in. I have never been good with directions. And I would never forgive myself if something bad happened to Willow under my guidance.

"Here!" Olivia cries out, skidding to a halt. She yanks on the door handle, but it doesn't budge. I push past her and drive my shoulder into it. It jolts but doesn't open. Inside, Emily startles and stares at us with wide eyes.

"Jake?" Doctor Jane's voice rings through the room. She frowns as she hurries over to us. Ignoring her, I drive my shoulder back into the door over and over.

"We need to get in!" I shriek, "Open the door!"

"Jake, what are you..." The doctor starts but I spin around and pull the lanyard from her neck. She stumbles forward in shock and grabs her neck protectively. I thrust the key against the lock. Slowly, the door opens.

"Get back!" Olivia shrieks as she flies towards Emily. I look at my sister. She is pale and sweaty, and unconscious. My heart drops in my chest as I grab her hand. It's limp.

"It's too late." Emily grins. Behind me, Doctor Jane storms in. Her hands fly to her face as the beeping sound of the monitor flat lines.

"No." I whimper, "No, no, no!"

The doctor shoves past and starts drawing up needles and medicine. The tears stream down my face as I fall to my knees. I rest my head against my sister's arm and sob. It's too late. I'm too late.

"Where the fuck is he?" Olivia seethes. I ignore her and keep clutching onto my sister.

"I don't know what you're on about." Emily spits. My head tears up, "Why, Alice? What the fuck is wrong with you?"

"Do I know you?" She raises an eyebrow. My heart drops. She plays naïve. She really is a cold-hearted bitch. Suddenly, Olivia tackles her. I jump to my feet and block the door. The security and nurses rush to interfere in the commotion. Nobody will be coming in or out of this room until my sister makes it. And even then, Emily will be fucking lucky if she gets out of here alive.

# CHAPTER TWENTY-EIGHT

## Willow's Pov:

I tremble as my parent's flash in front of me. We are in a dark room. The only thing I can hear is the pounding of my unsteady heart. They glow slightly.

*"Willow." My mum's soft voice fills the silence. My stomach twists in my stomach. No hatred or rage seeps from her today. She stumbles towards me and pulls me into an embrace. Her usual vanilla smell fills my senses, and I can't help but sob. My Dad joins the embrace. For the first time in six months, the feeling of security and safety fills me.*

*"My darling girl." He chokes on a sob. I feel my mum shake as she also cries. The wet tears stain my shoulder, but I don't care. I have wanted to embrace my parents for over half a year.*

*"We are so sorry." My mum whimpers, "For the pain we've caused you."*

*I pull back slightly and shake my head.*

*"No, no, I deserved it." I start to say but my mum cuts me off, "No, Willow. We were never out to hurt you. We'd visit you during the day whenever Emily was around. We knew what she was capable of."*

"How?" I whimper, pulling my arms around myself. My mum's face lights up slightly as she chuckles.

"Willow, we are in your imagination. Deep down, you knew that you didn't cause the fire. And you knew it had to do with the pale monster which would visit."

I look at my dad and he peers at the ground guiltily, "I am sorry that I invited her into our home. Our life."

My mum never releases his grip. I look between them helplessly. How can my mum still love him even after his affair?

"Sometimes, you have to sacrifice your pride, your ego for the person you love." She whispers, cupping my cheek. I lean into her gentle touch.

"We all make mistakes. Your dad decided to seek the touch of someone else." She explains slowly, "It isn't his fault. We are human. We all have desires, no matter how wrong. Emily just took it too far. What was supposed to be a one-night stand, turned into something much more hideous. Black mail. Threats. Murder..."

The lump in my throat tightens. I think back to Mr Anderson. The forbidden desire between us. He made plenty of mistakes too. He lied to me, hid from me, allowed the world to think I was crazy. And now he is gone. I would go through that torture ten times just to bring him back to me. A tear slips down my face.

Suddenly, a flash of light ripples around the dark room. I bring my arm to my face to shield myself.

"Go, child." My dad smiles sadly, "Go and live a happy life. Happiness will free you from being plagued by frightening delusions. And Emily will not touch you anymore."

"I love you mum and dad." I sob, pulling them into one last embrace. With a shaky breath, I slowly pull away and tip toe towards the light. It stings my senses and makes me feel nauseous. Suddenly, the sound of steady beeping echoes through my ears.

"Willow?" Jake calls out, "Willow! Yes, that's it. Open your eyes!"

219

Groggily, my eyes flutter open. The world it too bright, it makes me wince. I peer around the room. My brother clings to me. His eyes are red and puffy, and snot dribbles from his nose.

"Willow!" He cries, "Oh, God! I thought I lost you. I am so sorry. I am sorry I didn't believe you!"

The lump in my throat stops me from talking. Instead, I place a weak hand on his arms to reassure him. Then, my head lulls to the right. Doctor Jane trembles as she removes the needle from my wrist. I don't even feel the sting. She places a hand against my head and sighs in relief.

"Welcome back." She grins. I try to give her a small smile, but it doesn't seem to work. Then the horror floods through me at the memory of Emily's confession. I shoot up in the bed but my brother and the doctor force me to lay down again.

"Rest, Willow." I hear Olivia's voice rings through the room. More tears flood down my face as I look at my friend. My real life friend.

"She's gone now. The police have taken her." Jake explains miserably. He plays with his fingers and bites his lower lip nervously.

"And Mr Anderson?" I squeak, "W-where is he?"

Olivia chokes on a sob. Desperately, I look around the room, "Did she say where he was?"

Everybody ignores me. The anger and despair fill me.

"Answer me!" I shriek, "Where is he? Where is Liam?"

"We don't know." Olivia squeaks, rushing to my side. She grabs my hand anxiously, "What did he say to you when he saw you last time? Maybe he gave you a hint?"

I frown in confusion and try to remember our conversation. That day was incredibly stressful with Emily drugging me soon after. I blink back the burning tears. It feels as though my heart has been burst in my chest.

"Help me up." I squeak, throwing my legs to the side. Doctor Jane tries to protest but I send her a warning look. Nervously, the doctor and my brother take me by either arm. When my feet touch the cold floor, my knees threaten to buckle.

"It's going to take time, Willow." My doctor says anxiously, "You almost died."

"But I'm back now." I snap, "And he's out there somewhere."

I take a couple shaky breaths and step forward. I buckle but quickly correct myself. Slowly, I pull away from their help and learn to walk again. My body heaves in exhaustion and pain but I will not rest until I find him.

"Willow, you have to try! Did he mention anything?" Olivia tries. I close my eyes and force myself to remember. It floods back slowly by slowly.

"We went to a field?" I whimper, "With a lake? With Ducks…"

"Lively Grove!" Olivia gasps, throwing her hands to her mouth, "Yes, of course!"

"What?" My brother frowns.

"It's his favourite place to go to when he's stressed! Maybe he's there?" Olivia shrieks.

My legs carry me quickly out of the door. The sickness rises in my stomach and the tears don't stop flooding down. The others quickly follow. However, I skid to a halt.

"Doctor!" I gasp, "Lola! You have to find her. Emily hurt her too."

My doctor's lips thin and she nods. Quickly, she turns and flees to find help. I continue my struggled journey to the car. I have never loved my brother's awful speeding driving before. The exhaustion pulls my body in and out of sleep. However, as soon as the car comes to a halt, I'm ready to go again.

Olivia races around and helps me out of the vehicle. Together, we limp up the field. The small tendrils of grass lick at my feet and tickle. An overpowering smell of damp mud and lavender fills my nose. I peer around at the beautiful place. All the memories from when we were here together floods back into my heart. My heart aches.

"This way." Olivia says, pulling me up the small hill. I stumble to the top and race towards the tree line. A dirty bench, the same one Mr Anderson described rests in the thicket. Low moaning starts to become audible. I feel sick as I approach it.

Then, I see him. The man I love cowers in a foetal position.

"Liam!" I cry out, dropping to my knees in front of him. Weakly, he lifts his head up to look at me. For a moment, a look of confusion ripples through his face. He scowls at me before his eyes flutter shut.

"No!" I squeak, pulling his head to my lap. And then I see it. A huge pool of blood pours from his stomach. My jaw drops and I jolt forward in fear. Olivia falls to the ground and applies pressure to the wound. My head feels fuzzy as I stare at the blood. I slowly feel myself slipping into a delusion.

*No!* I must stay strong. I must stay in reality for Mr Anderson.

But the world won't stop fucking spinning.

"Willow?" He whimpers. It pulls me straight back into real life. His trembling hand lifts up to my cheek and it cups it. One of my tears fall onto his forehead. I kiss it off.

"I love you." He says, "And I'm sorry. Sorry about everything."

"I love you too." I croak, holding his head firmly like my life depends on it. The world blurs around me. I can't hear anything other than him and his heartbeat.

"Don't apologise." I scold him, "It's not your fault."

"I came to find you yesterday, I promise." He whimpers before choking on blood. The sight sets me off again. I ground myself by clenching and unclenching my fists. Shaky breaths keep me in the moment.

"A-and then she found me first." He grumbles, "I don't remember how I got here."

Olivia places a hand to his head and hisses, "He's burning up and pale. This isn't good."

Mr Anderson smiles lazily up at me. I place a desperate kiss to his lips. My whole-body heaves as I sob, "No, you're going to be okay. Promise me?"

Slowly, he shakes his head.

"I can't promise that." He whispers, "But I can promise that you are the only woman I've truly loved. Emily drugged me into loving her. You? I can't explain it."

"Save your breath." I whimper, clutching to his face tighter. He gives me one last smile before choking on another cough. Blood splatters out and covers my hands. I hyperventilate.

"No, no, no!" I cry, "Stop it! Liam, stay with me!" Then, everything goes hazy as a rush of sound echoes around me.

# CHAPTER TWENTY-NINE

*Four months in the future.*

## Willow's Pov:

"I did it!" I shriek, bounding into my flat. Quickly, I brush off the snow from my boots before stumbling into the living room. My friends and family all tear their gazes up at me expectantly. I clutch the exam certificate in my hand.

"I did it! I got a 2:1! I passed, oh my god, I passed!" I scream out in excitement, thrusting the exam certificate in front of Liam's face. Instantly, he shoots upwards. His large arms wrap around me, and he spins us around. But he flinches, and falls forward, hand desperately grabbing his waist. I jolt and fuss over him.

"Shit, I'm sorry! Are you okay? Did you break the stitches?"

A small grin pulls on his lips as he peers up at me through low lashes.

"Unfortunately for you, I am not going anywhere." He pulls me back into an embrace, "The bitch missed the important organs."

I can't help but chuckle at his crude humour. It's the only way you can survive such trauma.

"Your result is amazing, Willow. You should be so proud of yourself." He presses a soft kiss to my forehead and the butterflies in my stomach go crazy. I shake my head slowly, "I couldn't have done it without you."

He pushes my chin up to maintain eye contact with me, "You could have. You just had to believe in yourself."

The blush attacks my cheeks. I can't stop the huge smile which covers my face. He stares down at me lovingly and presses his lips to my own. It feels as though the world around us has faded away. The only thing I can hear is my heartbeat in my ears, and the taste of him makes my head woozy.

"Well done, Willow." My brother pulls me from the daydream. Unwillingly, I put distance between Liam and me, and embrace my brother instead. Not wanting to miss out, Olivia quickly wraps her arms around us both too. My heart fills full of love in this moment. And then a sudden feeling of guilt swarms me. How can I celebrate when my dear friend is still in the mental health facility. My brother picks up on my concern.

"She is being released this week." He tells me with a huge grin. My jaw drops and my eyes are wide.

"Wait! Really? Oh my God that is amazing!" I stumble over my excitement, "We must have a party for when she gets out or something! I am *so* happy for her!"

The smile on my lips couldn't grow anymore even if I forced it too. Everything is slowly falling into place. Emily is in prison. Lola has been released from her own prison. I am in Liam's arms.

In the far corner of the room, my mother and father smile lovingly at me. They clutch each other's hands and beam proudly. They don't need to say anything, I can feel their joy. For a second, my heart constricts. They look just like they did prior to the fire.

Slowly, they turn to face each other. I watch as my parents share a small kiss before turning away from me. Then, they exit the flat. Neither one turns around to give me a last look, but they don't need to. I understand that this is a goodbye. I will not be seeing them around anymore. I have Mr. Anderson to protect me nowadays; their job is done.

A large smile coats my lips as I face Liam again. He cups my cheeks and presses a light kiss to my forehead.

For the first time in my miserable life, I feel truly happy.

*Who needs delusions when you have love?*

"I need to resubmit that essay." I tell Liam, pulling his hands into my own. He scowls down at me, face full of confusion.

I clarify my thoughts with a cheeky smile, "Perhaps my life isn't a constant room 101 after all. Maybe there is hope for broken people."

# ACKNOWLEDGEMENT

I would like to thank all my loyal readers. I love you and appreciate everything you do for me to make my dream come true!

I love reading comments (as i'm sure you'll know by now) so please take the time to leave a comment on Goodreads or Amazon, or feel free to message me on

tiktok: hollyguywrites

I would also like to thank my Twin Sister for helping me achieve my dreams.

# BOOKS BY THIS AUTHOR

## Delphi Deceived

I am cursed for eternity.
He is using me for his personal gain.
There should be nothing erotic between enemies. And yet there is.

Roughly six centuries ago, a war wrecked chaos in the kingdom of Heaven and Hell. Laws were written in the blood of those fallen in a desperate cry for peace. Restrict the Original Beings, force them into submission, and no more war or suffering would occur.

Ideal on paper. A death sentence for Delphi, the High Priestess of time and fortune.

And then things got worse for her.

Kidnapped by Power, the God of strength and power, she is forced to help him on a dangerous mission he refuses to disclose. Power is an allusive, mysterious, and ruthless Original Being, and nothing will get in the way of what he wants.
Even if that includes Delphi herself.

# BOOKS BY THIS AUTHOR

## Illegal Activities

After Maya is freed from the Russian Mafia prison, she falls into the arms of another Mafia boss- Alessio Morisso. She swore that she would never become a prisoner again, but after stirring up a war with her feisty and sarcastic attitude, she is no longer safe to return home. The only way to ensure her survival is to marry Alessio.

However, beautiful and bold Maya will not be an obedient little housewife. On the contrary, she wishes for control and to escape. But when the lines blur between wanting to escape and desiring her new husband, Maya finds herself doubting everything she knew about herself.
Could she really resist his charms or must she join forces with him to take revenge against the Russians?

Read for a humorous and powerful female lead with an possessive, alpha male.

## Five Red Flags

She is a hard-working Bubble member. He is a blasphemous Freedom Fighter. Yet they both end up in the Red Flag Trials, fighting for their lives against the impossible odds.

Set in the year 2202, cancel culture is potent. The ruling elite had to prevent the misery and despair which wrecked their cities. Offence had to go. Change needed to happen. Happiness must be restored.

Once a diligent young worker, Arabella's perfect life crashes and burns when she first meets the new and intimidating arrival to her bubble- Isaac. His scandalous words and promises eventually land them into trouble with the ruling elite's new rules.

Forced to compete in a series of death trials with five other disgraced bubble members, Arabella can't help but question why she strayed from her perfect life beforehand. As each trial passes, the people around her that she grew to trust, wither away. Fear and friendship are indistinguishable in the Red Flag Trials, and hope is nothing but a four-letter word whispered in the dark.

Despite all this, Arabella can't help wondering what the bigger threat is... The trials themselves, or her mysterious lover who seems a little too knowledgeable about them.

## Deaths New Pet

A revenge-driven woman. A bitter Death-incarnate. And the Death Trials.

The Devil decides Death needs a new pet to keep him company in Hell. The way to find the perfect candidate: through a series of deadly trials to whittle ten mortals down to one. The winning human will be able to make a deal with the Devil.

Scarlet Larson enters the trials with the intent to make her abuser suffer. She desperately craves revenge against the man who held her hostage for eight years. However, as each trial passes, she begins to lose focus as she engages in a steamy love affair with Death.

She knows she should stop. She knows she should concentrate on the trials. But how can you say no to Death when he tempts you?

However, as the mortal begins to develop immortal powers, Death, alongside his Hellish family, begin to wonder who, or what, is Scarlet Larson?

## Please Don't Make Me Kill Him

My caring Lucius, my hateful Toby, and the wicked choice between them

Isla Morris, alongside her brother and father, are contracted killers. Their job includes infiltrating their target's lives to gain more information and then make a clean kill, all in the name of profit. However, when Isla falls in love with the man she is supposed to murder, trouble stirs.

Will she choose to stick to the mission, or will she betray her family in the name of love?

In the future, her decision haunts her in a new mission. And when a handsome, menacing stranger threatens to reveal all of her secrets, she must make more fateful choices.

With a blooming love triangle and everyone around her turning out to not be who she expected, Isla finds herself lost and in despair. She was supposed to play them, but now all the men in her life are playing her...